THE
VISITOR

by
P. Pikkert

CAN Books

PO Box 146, Beaconsfield, HP9 2GX., UK

ISBN 0 900828 81 1

To Anna,

who gladly follows me anywhere…

With special thanks to
William Kennedy and Betsy Hunter
for their invaluable critiques
of the manuscript.

The prayers I make will then be sweet indeed
If Thou the Spirit give by which I pray:
My unassisted heart is barren clay,
That of its native self can nothing feed:
Of good and pious works Thou art the seed,
That quickens only where Thou say'st it may:
Unless Thou show to us Thine own true way
No man can find it: Father! Thou must lead.
Do Thou, then, breathe those thoughts into my mind
By which such virtue may in me be bred
That in Thy holy footsteps I may tread;
The fetters of my tongue do Thou unbind,
That I may have the power to sing of Thee,
And sound Thy praises everlastingly.

Michael Angelo (1475-1564)
tr. William Wordworth (1770-1850)

Chapter 1

By the time the bus finally descended the ravine into town it was dark. Its whining, high-pitched engine struggled to keep it in check. Suddenly the road levelled, the driver moved up a gear and the engine resumed its steady, reassuring rumble.

The headlights probed the darkness, the moving strobe of light illuminating one squat, ramshackle building after another, until it shot out over a dark, open area. The driver downshifted once again and pulled into a gravel parking area. The lights fell on a grimy sign dangling from a forlorn, hutch-sized, cinder-block and corrugated iron construction: The South-East Bus Company, Hamadiye Office, it said.

Only the foreigner got off. The others stared mutely as he stood up, walked towards the front door, nodded at the driver and stepped into the darkness. He slung his bag over his shoulders and walked into the night, thirty pairs of eyes following him from the safety of the brightly lit bus.

The doors slammed shut, a hydraulic pump hissed, the engine revved and tyres crunched on the gravel. Increasing speed slowly the bus passed him, its cabin lights left on invitingly. Robert could see thirty heads craning backwards, staring at him.

The bus slipped onto the main road. Its dark mass dimmed rapidly and its drone grew fainter and fainter until only the little red tail-lights remained visible. Then they shrank and disappeared, and it was gone. It would arrive in Diyarbakir, the provincial capital, sometime after midnight.

Robert was left alone. A thrill of excitement pumped adrenaline to his extremities, pushing him along as briskly as he dared on the uneven ground. He knew his ebullience was a cheap, baseless thrill, but it was there and he savoured it. For the next twenty-four hours he would be the only foreigner in this insignificant, infamous little border town.

The fact that the town had a bad reputation appealed to him. When he had passed through on previous occasions he remembered thinking that the place actually looked ominous, probably because it was located in a narrow valley with a brooding, black-basalt castle, which the Turkish army used as an observation post, overlooking it.

Inge's disapproval perversely heightened his enjoyment of the moment. The poor, stressed-out woman lived in constant fear of the most remote possibility of what might overcome a man on the road. She was convinced that sooner or later he would be kidnapped, murdered, or seduced.

True, the newspapers were full of lurid stories about this part of the country, but it was a huge area and he'd never felt seriously threatened before. Only once was one of her improbable fears, the last one, nearly realised. And since she was incapable of understanding – let alone forgetting – that incident, she insisted that some other missionary accompany him on his treks, someone who would keep an eye on him for her. In spite of her nagging, however, he still set off alone as often as he could.

He liked being alone. There was something special, something romantic about walking alone at night in places like this God-forsaken, unimportant town. It wasn't the same when one of the others accompanied him. True, they were full of zeal, but they looked and acted like the foreigners they were. They spoke the language badly and were insensitive to the culture. It was impossible to keep a low profile with one of them around, and in places such as this town sensitivity to the culture and a low profile were essential. Inge wouldn't, couldn't understand that. How could she? She seldom accompanied him anywhere; she couldn't be expected to understand.

When he'd set off on this trek almost a month ago she had once again uttered her resentment in her usual, grating, insinuating way. He was pleased with himself for not caving in to her. He was becoming his own man again.

He smiled, and the darkness masked the bitter lines which etched his face whenever he thought of home. He couldn't postpone returning to Inge's rigid, frigid ways much longer. His make-belief adventures would end soon. But, praise God, there was still tomorrow. ...

He walked steadily toward the centre of town, vaguely aware of the flat-roofed, thick-walled stone and mud houses stacked one above the other on the steep slopes on either side of the road. The darkness and the outlines of the buildings blurred indistinctly. Here and there a curtain was left open, but the dull light from the low-wattage bulbs inside was incapable of penetrating far into the blackness. Once or twice he looked through a window and saw some people silhouetted like characters in a shadow play, their outlines moving before a rectangular patch of dull light. He heard a man raise his voice and he heard a woman shout angrily in reply. He couldn't make out what they said.

Although it wasn't late, it was already very dark. There was no moon, clouds hid the stars, and the steep hillsides prevented any light there might have been on the fringes of the night-sky from illuminating the bottom of the valley. He could see just far enough ahead to navigate the side of the road without stepping into the open sewer. Yes, he thought again, there was something romantic, something delicious, about being by yourself in a hostile environment.

Not that this place was really hostile; it was merely perceived as such. People at home thought of him as heroic because he liked trekking by himself in places perceived to be dangerous but weren't really dangerous at all. Although he knew he'd never done anything heroic, it was nice to think that others thought he had, even if they were only the members of his church back in Canada.

He wished he had been born in an era when one could be a missionary and an explorer at the same time. He would have become the Livingstone of the Middle East. He'd have become a Christian Burkhart discovering Petra or a Burton or Bruce exploring the source of the Nile, or a Clapperton or Caillie, a Park or a Laing traversing the length and breadth of the Sahara desert. A century or two ago being a missionary still had social prestige. ... Still, he was thankful that he wasn't born a decade or so later. At least there were still a few places like this where one could pretend to be a pioneer.

He reached a curve and spotted a lonely street light dangling limply from a wonky telephone pole up ahead. He assumed that it marked the main intersection, and quickened his pace to reach it.

It sure was dark tonight, he thought again. Dark as a root cellar. Although it was dark, it couldn't be much past 7.30pm Funny that there was no-one about. Maybe there was a curfew on, in which case he'd better find a hotel before the police found him.

He reached the wonky telephone pole, stood in the dim circle of light beneath it and peered up and down the intersection. About fifty meters up the road on the opposite side of the street a window at street level threw a shaft of light onto the pavement. It cast just enough light to illuminate a sign jutting from a building: Hotel Aktamar, it said. Relieved, he walked briskly, leaning forward to compensate for the upward angle of the road.

The stores leading up to the hotel entrance were shuttered. Mournful music accompanied the shaft of light, which turned out to be a tea-house. He could see a dozen men gathered around small tables playing cards, watching TV, and sipping tea. So there was no curfew – at least not this early. The tea-house looked inviting, but he knew he was too tired to answer awkward questions intelligently. He pushed through the hotel door and walked up the dusty, crumbling staircase to the foyer on the second floor.

Chapter 2

His name, Masoud, means 'happy'. It was, essentially, an appropriate name although that was not immediately evident because of his sober, thoughtful personality. He was sensitive, patient and concerned about the feelings of others. At odd times, however, his reserved, perceptive demeanour could be shattered by unexpected flashes of humour.

Like millions of young fellows before him he was drafted into the army. He suffered through boot camp in central Anatolia and then got a lucky break, although he didn't realise just how lucky a break it was until much later: he was transferred to a base just outside of Istanbul. There he spent sixteen tedious months guarding the main entrance to the base or patrolling its outer fence. It would probably be the only time in his life that the fact that he was Kurdish worked in his favour: the military didn't trust him enough to make him serve in the volatile Eastern provinces. The task of controlling the Kurdish population there was entrusted to loyal Turks from the West of the country.

Gate-duty, which was shared with another soldier and involved checking the ID papers and contents of vehicles entering the base, was tolerable. Guarding the outer fence, however, was another story. The soldiers doing guard duty there were strung along at half-kilometer intervals and weren't allowed to approach the next guard, since that could leave a kilometer wide gap.

Masoud spent most of his military career either freezing or frying along that fence, depending on the season. He was rained on, hailed on and snowed on. Other than changes in the weather, however, nothing remotely exciting happened during that entire period. But he faithfully kept his eyes open for interminably long stretches of time; failing to do so would have meant big trouble.

Although no exciting shoot-outs or guerrilla attacks took place while he stood on guard along that outer fence, the experience confronted him for the first time in his life with

the alien and terrifying emotion of loneliness. Never before
had he been forced to spend extended periods of time
utterly alone. The eery solitude he experienced while pacing
along that lonely stretch of fence pressed on his chest like a
dreadful weight. Furthermore, as he paced up and down his
little stretch of fence, his mind kept conjuring up variations
of the same nightmare, a nightmare whose recurring theme
was the horror of being bereft of his family. He envisaged
himself alone, lost, forgotten in the huge metropolis of
Istanbul.

His loneliness was exacerbated by the fact that he was
not only the only Kurd, he was also the only Alawite[1] in his
platoon. The others treated him like a leper and he felt very
vulnerable. Loneliness, he discovered, was a terrible thing.

Back at home in Hamadiye loneliness was an emotion
which simply didn't exist. Houses there were too small and
families too big for people to be able to afford the luxury of
solitude, a luxury which, in any case, people preferred to do
without. At home one's wider family was everything. It
supported, nurtured, moulded, enveloped and encom-
passed the individual. It was a shelter in times of storm and
a sanctuary from the law. It shared the burdens of hospitality, extended help in case of conflict and succour in times of
need. The thought of being left alone was inconceivable.
Even shepherds went out in twos! It was the height of rude-
ness to leave a guest unaccompanied. The worst fate which
could befall someone was to be rejected by one's family – a
fate which, fortunately, was reserved only for those foolish
enough to turn their backs on Islam.

As the weeks and months of Masoud's enlistment
slipped by, however, the intense imaginations and eerie fears
abated, although the oppressing sense of loneliness would
return forcefully at the oddest moments.

When off duty he took every opportunity he could to
explore the glitter and glory of Istanbul. He wandered
around the majestic mosques of the Sultan Ahmet square
and got lost in the labyrinthine Covered Market. He took

1. Partisan of the Caliph Ali.

the bus across the Golden Horn and visited the night clubs in Beyoglu. He would hop onto whatever ferryboat happened to be leaving Sirkeji and sail to wherever it happened to go – to the Asian side of Istanbul, to one of the Princess Islands, or up the Bosporus.

One day he discovered the used-book stores near the Galata tower and bought some old, black-and-white comic strips to help him pass the time. When he was through with them he sold them back to the store and bought a novelette, and when he'd read it he traded it in for a full-length novel. That was how he discovered the joy of Turkish literature. He escaped many a lonely, off-duty hour into the exciting, tragicomic worlds created by Aziz Nesin and Yashar Kemal.

On sunny summer weekends he liked to sit in one of the street cafés, sip a glass of tea and watch Istanbul's millions swirl past. Elegant business men in expensive suits would stride along purposefully, speaking authoritatively into puny pocket telephones. Pale, overweight, Western tourists draped in gaudy shirts and oversize shorts and clutching expensive cameras milled around aimlessly. They were trailed by bedraggled street-urchins, whose specialties ranged from looking doleful, holding out their grubby little hands and saying 'money for bread' in a dozen different languages, to pickpocketing. Impoverished street vendors hawked wares no one wanted, shark-like salesmen railroaded the unsuspecting into expensive little shops, and lithe girls wearing sleeveless tops which left their bellies naked and tight trousers which emphasised their sensuous curves paraded past, their hips swinging, their eyes sparkling, their hair swirling. If one of his sisters appeared like that in public, Masoud thought, he or one of his brothers would have been obliged to shoot her in order to salvage the family's honour.

He compared the huge metropolis' history-filled sprawl, its hustling, throbbing, pulsating streets, its magnificent architecture and bustling Bosporus to dreary Hamadiye which, though famous in Kurdish history, meant nothing to the millions around him.

Wedged in its stifling valley and straddling its dirty little river, Hamadiye was caught between a Kurdish insurrection born of hopelessness and the military's brutal response born of frustration. The generals, incapable of grasping that their onerous ways merely radicalised the population even more, responded to each outrage with an outrage of their own. But, like a spring pressed down only to pop up as soon as the pressure slackened, the people inevitably struck back: a mine would blow up a troop transporter, a sentry would be shot in the back, a hand grenade would be tossed into a restaurant filled with off-duty soldiers, or a Molotov cocktail lobbed into a passing jeep. The army would respond by shooting some suspects, stuffing yet more people into the jam-packed jails and imposing yet another curfew during which frustrated husbands and their haggard wives would generate yet more malcontented children to take the place of those they had lost. The tighter the military screwed on the lid, the more violent the ensuing eruption. It was a vicious, endless spiral.

But, in spite of everything, Hamadiye was home. He knew its every alley and every valley. His mother and father, his brothers and sisters, his cousins, uncles, aunts – his whole extended family – was waiting for him in Hamadiye. It might be an ugly, ignominious little town, but it was home. As he quietly sipped his tea and watched the throng around the St Sophia and the Blue Mosque, the loneliness and homesickness would tighten like a constricting belt around his chest.

While wandering around the city during his off-duty hours and while standing at his lonely post and staring at the high-rise apartment buildings and factories in the distance, Masoud began contemplating his future. He was torn by conflicting temptations: should he try his luck here in Istanbul? But he had no particular skills, and the fast pace and instant demands of the big city threatened him. Although the great city was fun to explore, and even though its masses of people, its used-book stores and its cheap cinemas gave him glimpses into a new, exciting and titillating world, he sensed instinctively that the inviting metropolis throbbing dully around him would use and discard him, a simple, Alawite, Kurdish country boy.

One chilly winter morning while he was stamping his feet futilely against the all-pervading dampness along the outer fence, Masoud's eyes fell on the smoke and tongues of fire which erupted periodically from the smoke stacks of the ramshackle leather tannery which adjoined the base at the point where he was standing. He had stared at its tiled roofs and yellowed walls many times before. Today, however, the place looked inviting. Those tongues of fire leaping from their chimneys suggested warmth and cosiness inside.

A truck pulled up to one of the buildings. The driver disembarked, walked up to a door and knocked. After a moment the door slid open and some other men appeared. Masoud could see them talking and laughing, although the sound was lost across the distance. Gently rolling opaque clouds of steam billowed from the open door. The driver opened the back of his truck while the others disappeared inside. They soon re-appeared carrying large bundles which they threw into the vehicle. The driver and another man climbed into the back, apparently to stack the bundles. It took them about half an hour to load it.

Masoud followed their every movement. He saw their friendly banter, saw someone coming with a tray of tea-glasses, saw them standing around the tail-gate sipping the hot-liquid and saw them get back to work. When they finished the driver signed some papers, climbed into the cab and, with a friendly wave, drove off. The others disappeared inside and the big door slid shut. A last cloud of vapour escaping from inside curled upwards and disappeared.

Watching the friendly, unhurried bantering of the workmen increased Masoud's sense of loneliness. He paced up and down restlessly, first looking intermittently, then long and hard at the leather factory.

Chapter 3

The staircase angled steeply up to the second storey where it ended in the middle of a hallway. When he got to the top Robert lowered his satchel to the ground and leaned on the rickety banister until his heart-beat and breathing resumed their normal pace.

He was hot; beads of perspiration trickled down his forehead. The swift climb up the hill and the steep staircase had winded him. He realised afresh that he was out of shape.

He looked around. White light filtering through double doors of unwashed opaque glass enabled him to make out the unmanned, dark wood sign-in desk across the hallway. A faded picture of Kemal Ataturk[2] and several rococo-like prints of flimsily clad houris, the perpetual virgins who serve the saved in the Muslims' paradise, adorned the walls.

The place smelled musty. Muffled sounds from a radio or TV. came from the direction of the light so he turned, walked down the corridor and opened the glass doors. A couple of stark neon lights illuminated a long, narrow room running parallel with the street for the width of the building. Six or seven men turned their heads away from a blaring television and looked at him with vaguely curious expressions on their faces.

'Good evening,' Robert said loud enough for everyone to hear above the noise of the TV. Several of the men nodded politely before shifting their gaze back to the screen. Robert's hair was dark enough and he knew the language well enough to be taken for a national in such a cursory scrutiny. He didn't actually look like a Turk, but he could pass as a Circassian or as a Laz[3].

'Is there anybody in charge of the desk?' he asked slightly louder than strictly necessary.

---

2. Founder of the Republic of Turkey.

3. The Circassians and the Laz are two different non-Turkic Muslim minority groups living in Anatolia.

A young man sporting a short-cropped, 'leftist' Che Guaverra beard roused himself from one of the overstuffed armchairs lining the back wall, ambled towards him and indicated with a nod that Robert should follow him. As they left the foyer and strolled back to the desk through the dim hall, Robert sized up the man. He looked like the typical frustrated, under-employed, leftist unable to save enough money for a dowry. If his beard had been long and shaggy and if he had worn a skull-cap he would have looked like the typical frustrated, under-employed Islamic fundamentalist unable to save money for a dowry.

The man reached for a switch and turned on the hall light. The neon tube responded reluctantly. Then he pulled the hotel registration pad and a sheet of carbon paper from a drawer, slipped the carbon paper into the pad and pushed it across the desk. He reached into the drawer again and fumbled around until he found a pen. Robert swung his satchel off his shoulder, lowered it to the ground, accepted the pen and filled in the appropriate blanks. The man stared passively into space. Robert completed the form in such a way that a superficial scrutiny wouldn't reveal the fact that the address was unintelligible; the pen left fortuitous blotches of ink on the paper. When he was finished he pushed the pad back across the desk.

'Your identification card,' the man asked flatly.

Robert handed the man his passport. The man looked at its deep-blue cover, flipped it open to the first page, read his name and looked up in surprise.

'You speak Turkish well for a foreigner.'

'I've hardly opened my mouth.' Robert allowed a twinkle to illuminate his eyes.

The man smiled. 'Have you been in this accursed country a long time?'

'I live in Istanbul.'

'What brings you to this god-forsaken town?' The man wasn't nosy, just curious.

'Adventure.'

The man smiled. 'A couple of weeks ago the guerrillas kidnapped a German tourist. He got more adventure than he bargained for.'

'A couple of weeks with the guerrillas must have been great for his Kurdish,' Robert replied blandly. The man's eyes widened slightly before involuntarily darting left and right to ascertain whether anyone was eavesdropping.

'Do you speak Kurdish?' he asked quietly.

'My friends taught me just enough to get me into trouble,' Robert said, lifting the corners of his mouth and eyes.

The man laughed. 'Well, you'd better speak Turkish around here, Mr …,' he lifted the passport and glanced at the first page again.

'Mr Robert.'

'I will.'

Robert felt good. He'd played his cards right. He'd judged the man astutely, established his pro-Kurdish sympathies and was rewarded with a warning: not everyone in the foyer could be trusted. At least this man wouldn't make life difficult for him, Robert thought. He might even come in handy in a difficult spot.

'Can I have my passport back?' Robert asked politely.

'Not yet. The military police haven't done their security check yet.'

Robert's heart sank. He'd hoped they'd have completed their customary check of hotels before his arrival. He'd be trailed tomorrow.

The man lifted a key from a pigeon hole in the wall behind him, walked around the desk, lifted Robert's satchel and headed for the staircase. They climbed the two remaining flights to the top floor in silence. A naked bulb suspended from a bare wire illuminated the stairwell. They walked a few metres down the murky hallway before the man pushed open a door, stepped into a room and turned the light on. Robert followed him inside.

A rusty steel-frame bed stood in a corner. Some blankets lay folded at the foot and a rickety chair stood at the head of the bed. The sheets were stained. Thick, dilapidated, grey curtains drooped from the ceiling like an elephant's hide and a chipped enamel sink hung slightly askew beside the door. Only the details distinguished this room from the hundreds of others he'd stayed in.

'Is there water?' Robert made a vague gesture toward the sink.

'Yes. The toilets and showers are at the bottom of the hallway. There is hot water from 7 to 10 in the morning.'

'When is breakfast?'

'Between 7 and 11.'

'Can I get something to drink in the foyer?'

'Yes. Beer, Tea, Cola, Fanta. Anything you want.'

'Good. I'll come down in a minute.'

The man nodded, dropped the satchel on the bed, handed Robert the key and left, closing the door behind him.

Chapter 4

The agonisingly lonely stretches of time Masoud spent on the streets of Istanbul and along the base's perimeter fence paid off in the end, for by the time he was discharged from the army he had it all worked out. The key to his future, he decided, was leather. While staring at those leather factories and thinking of home it slowly dawned on him that an opportunity awaited, an opportunity he could profit from.

The economy of Hamadiye, such as it was, rested on two pillars: opium and sheep. The mountain pastures which surrounded the town were ideally suited for the cultivation of opium poppies, which was a very lucrative but also very illegal business. The same mountain pastures were also suitable for raising sheep and goats, which was perfectly legal but paid peanuts. The poppies were bought up by furtive dealers, carted off to secret laboratories and transformed into pure, white, flat cakes which were transported in secret bus and truck compartments to Germany, France, Italy and Holland.

The sheep and goats, on the other hand, never left Turkey. They were either slaughtered and eaten locally or trucked to Diyarbakir and consumed there. The only time when the villagers made any profit from their sheep was during the annual feast of sacrifice when every Muslim, irrespective of whether he took his religion seriously or not, bought a sheep or a goat and sacrificed it to atone for his sins. Part of this sacrifice was eaten and part of it distributed among the poor. The innards were used for various types of tripe soup, the bones ground into fertiliser and the hides bought up by dealers who sold them to the leather tanneries in Istanbul. There they were transformed into handbags, briefcases, shoes, leather coats, belts, purses and key-chains.

The sheep-hide business was typical of the economic relationship between the undeveloped Kurdish East and the industrialised, Turkish West of the country: the East provided the raw materials for the West to develop and export. The finished products produced in the West were not only exported to Europe, but also transported back to the East to be sold to the local Kurdish population.

It took a long time for the uneducated Masoud to work it all out, but then he had lots of time on his hands. Eventually, however, he was led to ask the logical question, a question many intellectual Kurds, most of whom were either in prison or in exile in Europe, had posed before him: why could they not tan the local sheep, goat and cow skins in the East and make those purses, coats, shoes and hand-bags themselves?

The difference between Masoud and the imprisoned or exiled Kurdish intellectuals was that Masoud did not draw conspiracy theories and write critical articles for poorly printed left-wing journals. He merely saw an opportunity which spurred him to visit the yellowing leather-works with the tiled roof next to the base and get to know some of the workmen there. And when he visited the used-book shop down by the Galata tower the next time, he scoured the place for manuals on leatherworking.

Chapter 5

Robert sat on the edge of the chair and moved the heavy curtain a few inches to one side. The street was deserted and from his high angle he was unable to see into the lighted window of the teahouse across the road. If he pressed his face against the window, though, he discovered he could look back down to the wonky street light at the intersection at the bottom of the hill. He let the curtain drop back into place and flopped onto the bed.

He lay quietly for a minute. The bed was too soft; he'd probably have a backache in the morning. His body was tired, but because his mind was active he knew he'd be unable to sleep. His mind, usually good company during the daytime, often turned sour at night. If he tried to sleep now he'd just toss and turn and his thoughts would turn to home. That's why he told the man he would come down to the foyer for a drink.

As long as his mind behaved itself however, he didn't have to go down. His eyes travelled over the dirty smudges and patches on the ceiling. He figured that the dark yellow stains were the result of water leaking from the room above and the light yellow stains the result of time on cheap paint. The black spots were squashed flies and the red-and-black blotches squashed mosquitoes. He couldn't figure out what the brown streaks were.

His mind shifted into neutral, then locked onto his children. They would have had their bedtime story, said their prayers and be in bed. His little girl would be sleeping peacefully on the top bunk while his boy was reading by the little light he'd rigged up for him last month. In a few minutes Inge would whisper through the doorway that it was time to turn the light off.

Even if her control over the kids was too stifling, Inge was a good mother. The kids meant everything to her; she was determined they would be the success she once hoped he would be.

The day after tomorrow he'd have to return home. He simply couldn't postpone it any longer. He had to go back to her silent, undefined aura of condemnation and to her humourless, stifling German routines. He wished she were ugly, wished he weren't attracted to her unresponsive body. It was a small step from thinking about her attractive, unresponsive body to imagining some other attractive but enthusiastic woman walk up behind him, place her head between his shoulder blades, unbutton his shirt and run her hands over his body. ...

Robert sat up, sighed dispiritedly, and headed for the lobby.

Chapter 6

The modern Mercedes bus headed eastward. For about two hours it followed the coast road along the Sea of Marmara and then turned inland toward the Bolu mountains, that towering mass which separates Istanbul from Ankara. The spring rains had come and gone and the sun shone brightly. The mountains were startlingly green, their highest peaks bisected abruptly by the brilliant snow line.

The bus cruised through the mountain passes without difficulty, then began its descent to the Anatolian plateau. A tape of a man repetitively crooning up and down the complicated, microtonal eastern scale to the accompaniment of the lute, the kanun and the harpsichord, lulled the passengers into that dozy, cosy state which straddles sleep and daydreaming. The bus sped south-eastwards over the undulating double highway which spans the plateau between the mountains and Ankara, the capital city.

Six hours after leaving Istanbul the bus pulled into Ankara's modern three-tiered bus terminal. An hour later it resumed its journey. Other passengers had replaced those who'd disembarked in Ankara. The vehicle sped south passing through numerous villages and towns. The passengers caught glimpses of tractors ploughing dark, fertile fields, of squat women and lively children herding flocks of muddy sheep and of men sitting on low stools sipping tea from small glasses in the courtyards of tumble-down teahouses shaded by the lush red and purple blooms of Bougainvilleas.

The sun sank slowly below the horizon as the bus careered past the Great Salt Lake. The steward extracted the crooning tape from the cassette recorder and popped a video into the VCR. For two hours a comedian held everyone's attention, and then the bus pulled into another road-side restaurant. After a late supper and refuelling they set off once again. This time the steward dimmed the lights and people nodded off, some snoring soundly, others twisting and turning uncomfortably in their seats in an effort to exercise stiff necks and sore butts. The steward stretched out in the empty space between the back seats and the back window and was soon fast asleep.

The bus came to the end of the Anatolian plateau and the driver, smoking one cigarette after another, navigated the bus around the dark hairpin turns high above the crevasses and ravines of the Taurus mountains. By the time the first light broke over the horizon they had crossed the mountains and were speeding over the fertile Chukurova plain toward Adana, Turkey's cotton capital, and gateway to the East.

The steward woke up, crawled out of his bunk, stumbled to the front of the bus and got a bottle of cheap cologne from the glove-department. Then he walked up and down the aisle, woke up the passengers and offered them a shot of the pungent fluid to rub onto their faces and necks. He came around a second time with a thermos of hot water and little plastic bags containing a tea-bag, a packet of sugar and a piece of dry cake. By the time the passengers had consumed the beverage and eaten the cake the bus was rolling through the outskirts of Adana.

The minute the bus pulled to a stop in the city's sprawling terminal it was overrun by ragged children carrying trays of freshly made cheese-and-tomato buns, frustrated young men peddling cheap watches and disillusioned old men trying to sell second-hand waistjackets and coats.

Along with the other passengers Masoud descended from the bus and stretched his legs. He bought a bun from a child and a glass of tea from a wandering tea-salesman. No-one paid him any attention as he squatted against a wall in his baggy, comfortable 'shalwar' trousers, striped dress shirt, threadbare waistjacket and workman's cap. He looked exactly what he was: a young villager on the move.

At any one time there were tens of thousands of young men like him on the move across the country. The military operations in the East displaced masses of villagers, forcing them to seek their fortune in the harsh, unforgiving cities of

Western Turkey. In this way the military killed three birds with a single stone: it undercut support for the Kurdish guerrillas in the countryside, it forced the autarkic villagers into the market economy, and by first disowning and then redistributing their land in large sections to wealthy farmers, it rationalised agricultural production. The downside of this grandiose scheme was that the cities became a catchment area for countless desperate, dispossessed Kurdish villagers. The huge shanty-towns became hotbeds for urban terrorism. How the swollen, impoverished masses living there managed to feed themselves was a national mystery.

Squatting comfortably against a pillar and sipping his tea, Masoud watched the steward clean out the bus. He savoured the moment. All things good and bad eventually come to an end, he thought, even sixteen months of mind-numbing military service. He had said farewell to his uniform and late this afternoon he would be home.

In the East a man is not accepted as a fully-fledged member of society until he has completed his military duty, found employment, been married and had a son. He had successfully finished the first condition and the secret to the second condition lay wrapped in a couple of bundles and in a wooden box in the bottom of the bus. He shot a furtive glance in the direction of the closed cargo-bays and smiled. The third condition would take time, since he wouldn't have money for a dowry until he had successfully completed the second condition. That, however, didn't matter too much. Ayshe, the cousin his family had picked out for him was, at age 12, still a bit young.

Once again the PA system crackled, then announced that all those heading for Diyarbakir were to climb aboard. Masoud stood up, gestured to the tea-man, handed his glass back and paid the man. Then he climbed back onto the bus and returned to his seat. Once again new passengers replaced those who had reached their destination; there was only a handful of people left who, like Masoud, had begun their journey in Istanbul. A different driver and another steward climbed aboard for the long run to Diyarbakir.

The bus pulled out of its parking slot and headed for the terminal's main gate. A few minutes later it was speeding Eastward. For the length of the Chukurova Valley the road ran parallel to the Jeyhan river. Then, when the river was forced northwards by the Amanos Mountains, the bus dropped a gear to toil steadily through this formidable barrier which separates the high Anatolian plateau, the traditional homeland of the Hittites, Byzantines and Turks, from the much lower Mesopotamian plateau which, since time immemorial, was the home of Semitic peoples: the Babylonians, the Chaldeans, the Arameans, the Arabs and the Jews. Masoud looked with interest at the ruins of imposing Ottoman, Arab and Crusader castles which dotted the craggy hilltops, each a mute testimony to the violent history of the ancient trail the bus was following. The Silk Route wound and coiled across Turkey and Kurdistan to Persia, Afghanistan, India and, eventually, China. Today, along stretches of the old trail, a smorgasbord of guerrilla groups and their respective central governments fight for control among each other.

But it was not just the landscape that changed. Instead of villages made of solid concrete blocks and red roof tiles, the bus passed more and more hamlets made of mud-brick walls topped by thick flat roofs made of hard-packed dirt trampled onto tree-trunk roof beams. Horse-drawn carts and simple bullock-drawn ploughs took the place of tractors trailing multiple-point blades. Flashes of colourful Kurdish dresses replaced the drab browns and greys worn by conservative Turkish women. Khaki-uniformed, blue-bereted, tough-looking commandos peering from sand-bagged check-points replaced soft-bellied, blue-uniformed, middle-aged traffic policemen. Every so often the commandos stopped the bus and two or three of them would check everyone's identity papers.

By mid-morning the bus had reach Gaziantep, Turkey's smuggling gateway to Syria. During the early afternoon the bus snaked along the Syrian border to ancient Urfa, old Edessa, the city of the prophets. Here Abraham had buried his father Terah. Here, according to tradition, the devil had tempted Job. Here Kurd, Arab and Turk have intermingled for more than a millennium without losing their respective identities.

After Urfa the road curved north-eastward, skirting the Eastern Taurus mountains to the north and the Mardin Hills to the south. The bus rocked gently over the sloping hills toward Diyarbakir, the unofficial capital of Kurdistan. As the terrain grew hillier the military presence increased. Here and there Masoud caught glimpses of tanks and armoured personnel carriers draped in camouflage netting. The bus was stopped more frequently and the soldiers checking the identification papers became increasingly unfriendly.

Masoud's excitement grew with every kilometre the bus sped eastwards. The metamorphosing landscape and the glimpses of his own people struggling in their age-old patterns somehow confirmed to him that he had made the right decision. This was where he belonged, and not in some great, impersonal, Turkish metropolis. This was his country, these were his people, this was where his roots were, this was where, by God's grace, he was going to make a go of it.

They were approaching Diyarbakir's black basalt walls when they ran into another road block. After the usual identity check a sergeant made the steward empty the cargo bays. Everyone had to get off the bus and identify their baggage. The sergeant made his men rummage through the luggage of those whose faces didn't appeal to him. Masoud was last in line. He sat comfortably on his box, his oversized bundle beside him, and waited until the soldiers reached him.

'What's in there?' The sergeant said gruffly, pointing at the big bundle.

Masoud stood up. 'Leather, sir.'

'What's in that box?'

'Bottles of leather paint, twine, punches, scissors. There are also some books.'

'What kind of books?' the man asked suspiciously.

'Books about working leather, sir.' Masoud replied politely.

'Going into the leather-business are you?'

Masoud grinned sheepishly and nodded his head. The man smiled.

'Good luck,' he said. 'Reload the bus!' He shouted. 'Have a good journey.'

He and his men walked away from the bus and disappeared behind a double row of sandbags.

The steward threw the baggage back into the cargo-bays while the passengers got back on the bus. Masoud helped the man heave his bundles back into place before reboarding the bus and dropping into his seat. He calculated that it would be evening by the time he got home.

Chapter 7

Robert sauntered into the lobby slowly enough to get an idea of who was sitting where. Immediately to the right of the entrance stood a little steel desk at which the bearded hotel manager, who had earlier shown him his room, sat reading a newspaper. Between it and the wall was a soiled, dark green bar. A television hung suspended from the ceiling in a brown angle-iron frame in the far right corner. There were four low coffee tables placed at right angles to the opposite wall from where he was standing, with short, low couches on either side. No one was sitting at the first table, probably because it was too close to the overhead television. Four men wearing Arab kaffiyes were discussing something among themselves around the second table and the third table was also empty. Two Turks wearing baggy 'shalwar' trousers and a third man in a cheap suit occupied the fourth table. A clean-cut man in an open-necked shirt and wearing polished army boots occupied one of the three overstuffed chairs along the back wall. Robert assumed he was the secret service policeman on duty. They might wear civilian clothes, he thought, but they never took their boots off. Two white plastic tables with white plastic chairs stood along the wall immediately to the left of the doorway. Robert caught a glimpse of someone sitting at one of those tables as he walked past.

He strolled to the empty coffee-table between the four Arabs and the three Turks and sat down facing the television. However, he took care to lean his back against the wall and to throw his arm over the back of the couch so that he could take in the whole room without appearing to look over his shoulder.

With a hand-movement he drew the attention of the bearded manager.

'A Cola, please.'

The man nodded, stood up and walked to the bar. Robert watched him go. The rickety structure was crying out for a fresh coat of paint. A Tuborg beer tap protruded above the counter. Rows of transparent, smallish bottles with blue and white labels and filled with clear, colourless Raki, the powerful raisin based liquor which, when mixed with water, turned milky white and was commonly referred to as Lion's Milk, stood in neat rows on sagging formica shelves along the back wall. A couple of dusty bottles of Johnny Walkers and several brown, slim-necked bottles of Turkish wine towered over the Raki bottles.

Then Robert's eye fell on the aquarium. It was a home-made affair constructed from fluorescent green angle-iron and glass in which two or three oversized goldfish pushed languidly through slimy green water. A framed picture of a gorgeous blond in a skimpy white bikini reclining in a wicker chair and sipping something from a tall glass hung above it. The words 'Tuborg Beer' were written in large, black and gold Germanic fonts along the bottom of the picture. Robert's eye wandered towards the television and he caught a glimpse of a distraught woman pleading with a man on a horse.

The bearded hotel manager set a glass of Cola in front of him. Robert nodded and smiled at the man who nodded back and went back to his chair behind the desk. Robert lifted the glass to his lips and sipped slowly. The three Arabs at the table next to him appeared to be discussing the price of something. One of them was jabbing his finger at a calculator. All three had the typical hawkish, Semitic features of the Bedouin: lean bodies, shining black eyes set in a thinnish face, largish nose and exuding an aura of dignity and ignorance. Robert wondered if they were related. He figured that they must be in their forties and be Syrians, probably from Qamishly or Amuda, who had come to buy Turkish textiles, machine parts, electronic goods or lard. All three wore long, cream-coloured, dusty robes. Their heads were adorned with white kaffiyes folded in various ways and held in place by the round, black cord of the egal[4]. Bare feet in sandals completed their outfit.

4. Arab headdress consisting of square cloth and round, black band.

There was something attractive about Arabs, Robert mused. Unlike Turks, who seemed to suffer from a national inferiority complex, Arabs exuded self-confidence. Only a Turk, for instance, would ask which country you liked better, your own or Turkey. Turks seemed to crave the approval of Westerners while exhibiting a national urge to extol their nation's presumed virtues to anyone with ears to listen: Turkey's cuisine was the world's best, its mountains, beaches and forests incomparable, the hospitality and friendliness of its people renowned and its historical sites the best preserved anywhere. The reason the country had a bad image was because there was a Greek-Slavic-Arab-Persian-Kurdish-Armenian-Christian-Free Mason conspiracy which endeavored to undermine Turkey's standing abroad, and because its politicians were unable to exploit the country's potential. After lauding his country ad nauseam the average Turk would then inquire how he could immigrate to the West. It was pathetic, really. Robert wondered if the reason Turks were ill at ease with themselves was because at a gut level they knew that no one but they themselves accepted their sectarian version of history – that the Armenian genocide was really the story of vile fifth-columnist Armenian militants killing innocent Turks, and that the ungrateful Arabs should be grateful for centuries of enlightened Ottoman rule. It really was pathetic.

It wasn't that he disliked Turks. Not at all! After all, they were his best friends and worst enemies.

But Arabs were different. Their history consisted of empires which had reached the height of refined civilisation and of great leaders overcoming the legacy of countless incompetents. Their deserts had nurtured prophets and their language was as pure and vast as the Empty Quarter. Arabs had nothing to hide; their past and present follies and feats were common knowledge and left them secure in the superiority of their ways.

Robert had to smile as the man who had done the calculations triumphantly waved the calculator in front of his two friends' noses. They leaned back thoughtfully. He had evidently made a point.

Robert took another sip of his Cola and then turned slightly to look at the men behind him. They were watching the television. He accidentally locked eyes with the man wearing the cheap suit but broke the spell by nodding pleasantly. The man nodded back. He looked every part the Turk he was: a short, squat body, a square face, eyes set far apart and with a slight Oriental touch. It was a Genghis Khan type of face that could metamorphose from exaggerated friendliness to extreme cruelty in a moment. The other two were engrossed in the film. In their workmen's caps, shabby waistjackets, baggy 'shalwar' trousers and slip-on shoes, they looked like they might be truck drivers.

Robert glanced over to the overstuffed armchairs, to what he presumed was the policeman. The man looked like a Turkish version of Jean Claude Van Damme: muscular, square faced, short-cropped hair, wearing blue jeans, a sports shirt and army boots. Robert thought he could see a bulge under the arm-pit where the man appeared to keep a pistol. Although he too was watching the television, Robert sensed that nothing escaped his notice.

Robert surreptitiously shifted his glance to the man sitting at the plastic table across from him. He was heavy-set and powerful looking. His ample stomach flowed over his belt, putting the shirt-buttons under considerable strain. With one beefy, greasy hand he was absentmindedly swirling a half-full glass of milk-white raki. He seemed to be staring at the girl in the white bikini on the Tuborg advertisement.

Robert's eyes flitted past the man at the desk, past the bar and aquarium to settle on the television. A man on horseback was chasing a girl down a steep incline. He was waving a shotgun. The horse skidded on the loose gravel and the man laughed boisterously. Then the camera closed in on the girl. She was running for her life, slipping and sliding down the slope. She ran barefoot, holding her skirt up with one hand. Her legs were scratched, dusty, exquisite, their muscles taut, straining. Beautiful, long, wild, unkempt black hair bobbed and bounced as she turned her head this way and that, looking wildly in every direction, searching for a way of escape. Her eyes were large with fear. She glanced back at the man on the horse, tripped and fell. The man laughed raucously as he closed in on her. She leapt to her feet and dived into a thicket of bramble bushes. The thorns tore at the clothes on her body. The camera zoomed in; the woman was beautiful, beautiful like a hunted animal was beautiful. Everyone stared at her.

With almost superhuman effort Robert tore his eyes away. They landed on the Tuborg advertisement. Oh God, help! The aquarium! Look at the aquarium! The woman panted desperately, the man laughed evilly, the horse snorted.

Suddenly the lobby door opened wide. Two blue-bereted commandos entered and looked around the room. The manager got up from behind his desk and headed for the door. The soldiers turned around to follow him. Robert noticed, however, that as they left one of them looked at the obese man sipping raki across from him. The man responded with just a trace of a smile.

Good night, Robert thought. That fat slob is the police informer, not that Rambo with the shiny boots! Suddenly he felt very tired. His eyes strayed back to the television screen. The woman was on her knees in the dirt, begging for mercy. She crouched forward and clasped the man's boots. He looked down at her and his tongue flickered at the edges of his mouth, his lips curled upwards. The horse grazed peacefully.

Robert stood up and headed for the door. The commandos were going through the hotel register. He nodded at then.

'Have a good evening'.

They nodded back.

'You too.'

Chapter 8

Home! His father, brothers, sisters and numerous cousins came to the bus-stop in Uncle Mehmet's truck to meet him. There were hugs, kisses and tears all around and then they piled into the truck and cruised around town waving flags and blaring the horn. One of his cousins beat lustily on a huge drum and another one played the zurna[5], his cheeks bulbous and his brow furled in concentration as he improvised an endless, uninterrupted, joyous wail. When they eventually arrived in their quarter the whole clan was there to welcome him back. More cousins and uncles pumped his arm and kissed him while the women uttered happy, high-pitched trilling noises.

Father, standing proudly beside him, nudged him through the crowd toward home while his brothers lugged his parcels from the truck into the house, wondering about their contents. When he got home his mother fell on his shoulders and wept with joy. Masoud kissed her hands and tears of joy came to his eyes. It was wonderful to be reunited with his family.

The men took their shoes off and headed for the living room. Masoud moved to his customary place to the right of the mattress and pillows reserved for the head of the household and honoured guests, but his father would have none of it. He insisted that his son take the place of honour in the middle of the mattress, the place farthest removed from the doorway. Masoud refused politely of course, insisting that his father take the seat of honour. He would be content to sit at his father's right side.

One of his sisters spread a large plastic table cloth on the floor and the male members of the family and old friends, sitting cross-legged, gathered around it. The sister then placed several dishes filled with pistachio nuts, almonds, salted pumpkin and watermelon seeds on the plastic sheet along with several small bowls of rock sugar. Then she

5. A kind of recorder.

poured tea into little glasses which she handed to father who passed them all around, beginning with Masoud. The men reached for the sugar bowl, placed a lump of sugar between their teeth and sipped their tea through it.

They brought Masoud up to date with the local gossip, swapped army stories and told of journeys they'd taken. No matter how involved he was in a conversation, Masoud's father kept a close eye on his guests' tea-glasses. Without asking he would signal his daughter who would re-fill them when they were close to becoming empty. After two or three glasses of tea the men indicated that they had had enough by turning their glass on its side or by putting a tea-spoon on top of it and placing their right hand over their hearts.

Father eventually collected the glasses and handed them to a daughter who soon re-appeared with a huge round tray piled high with rice, pine-nuts, aubergine, and deliciously spiced mutton. Another daughter brought in a pile of plates which father filled to overflowing.

Eating is serious business. The men fell silent as they lifted their spoons and turned towards their plates. It would be rude to distract anyone from eating. Only the giggling coming from the pile-up of shaven children's heads with their laughing, naughty, brown eyes which filled the doorway, the titter emanating from the women in the kitchen, the quiet crunching sounds and the odd belch disturbed the hallowed silence.

Suddenly there was a stir in the hallway. The kids who had filled the doorway scattered and a sister appeared in the opening gesticulating nervously. Masoud's father jumped up and left the room, to reappear a moment later ushering in Uncle Mehmet's massive bulk. Masoud jumped up and kissed the man's pudgy hand. The rest of the men shuffled to their feet while Uncle Mehmet nodded and smiled, his massive face creasing. He told everyone to sit down and carry on. The men were careful to sit slightly down from where they had been sitting, so there would be room on the cushion in the place of honour. Masoud moved to the right and his father to the left and Uncle Mehmet took his seat between them. A sister appeared with another plate to be filled to overflowing.

Uncle Mehmet was their quarter's Mukhtar, their representative to the local authorities. He was their clan's richest and most important man. His presence was an unexpected honour.

Throughout the meal, Masoud's father attended to his guests. It was, after all, a privilege to serve; no guest should be dishonoured by having to attend to his own needs. As the mound of food on the guests' plates decreased he would, without asking, pile on another generous quantity. Verbal refusals were not taken seriously; they were merely polite expressions of courtesy. It wasn't until a guest pushed his plate away from himself or covered it with his hands and said a closing blessing that one could be sure he was sincerely refusing any more food. All the while father deliberately paced his own eating to the speed of the slowest guest so that that individual would not be left eating alone.

Eventually everyone, even Uncle Mehmet, had had enough. They all sat back, rubbed their distended stomachs, belched, grunted and murmured blessings on the family. One of Masoud's sisters reappeared, collected the tray and hauled it off to the kitchen so the women and children could dine on the leftovers.

Masoud made a surreptitious gesture to a younger brother, one of the boys who had unloaded his box and bundles from the truck. The teenager jumped up from his place near the door at the bottom of the hierarchical seating arrangement and made his way to Masoud. Masoud whispered something in his ear whereupon the boy fetched the smaller of Masoud's bundles. Imitating his father's deliberate dignity Masoud slowly opened it. First he extracted a beautifully inlaid backgammon board which he handed to Uncle Mehmet.

'Masoud! You shouldn't have! I spend too much time in the tea-house as it is!' The huge man cried and proceeded to shake his head and murmur indignantly about how totally unnecessary this was. Uncle Mehmet was obviously pleased.

Masoud then extracted various other presents from his bag. A beautifully carved wooden Qur'an stand for his father and various smaller souvenirs for his brothers and sisters. For his mother he had a roll of lovely bright red cloth with bold yellow stripes and a golden thread woven through it. When the woman appeared in the men's room to receive it there were tears in her eyes. The men murmured approvingly. After the presents were handed out a sister lugged in trays of apples, pomegranates and grapes and Masoud's father handed small plates and knives all around.

Masoud's eyes travelled around the circle. Uncle Mehmet was peeling an orange, his vast bulk heaving and wheezing. Ahmed, who took religion seriously and felt it was his duty to steer the family toward religious orthodoxy, now boasted a wispy beard. He looked as intense as ever. Next to him sat Ayhan, the playboy, always ready with a joke, always winking at the girls. Someday, Masoud thought, he would overstep the bounds with some Sunni[6] girl and her brothers would beat the living daylights out of him.

Bahadir was discussing the latest political developments with Mehmet. Mehmet worked in the city hall and was expected to keep his ears open.

It was good to be home. This was where he belonged. This was his clan, these were his family. Among them he was a Kurd among Kurds, an Alawite among Alawites. These people meant security; he loved them and meant something to them. By God's grace he wouldn't let them down.

---

6. Sunni is the main, 'orthodox' branch of Islam.

Chapter 9

It was 11.00pm when Robert returned to his room. He flopped onto the bed, extracted a small Sony short-wave radio from his satchel and turned it on in time to catch the BBC's reassuring call signal. He fine-tuned the instrument and placed it on the chair beside his bed. Then he kicked off his shoes, stripped down to his underwear, turned the light off and stretched out on the sagging mattress.

'Good evening. I'm Sandy Walsh. It is 8.00pm Greenwich Mean Time. This is News Hour on the BBC from London. Welcome to the programme.

'These are the hour's top news stories: Turkey has again invaded Northern Iraq in an attempt to eliminate bases belonging to the Kurdish Guerrilla movement, the PKK.

'The US coastguard discovered several tons of cocaine on a Panamanian registered cargo-ship intercepted on the high seas.

'Tamil Tiger guerrillas in the Jaffna Peninsula have overrun a police station. There are reports of many casualties.

'In a joint news conference PLO-leader Yasir Arafat and Israeli prime-minister Netanyahu reported progress in their fight against the Islamic fundamentalist group Hamas. Now for the news in detail:

'Turkish ground forces, supported by heavy artillery and air power, have again crossed the border into the Kurdish held enclave in Northern Iraq in a fresh attempt to eliminate bases run by the Kurdish guerrilla movement, the PKK As yet there are no reports of casualties. The PKK, which operates from the Syrian controlled Bekaa Valley in Lebanon, established a series of bases along Northern Iraq's border with Turkey in the aftermath of the Gulf War. From these bases the rebels organise raids into Turkey against both military targets and civilians it accuses of collaboration with the Turkish government. Both NATO and UN spokesmen have condemned the cross-border action and Germany has expressed concern that military hardware it sold to Turkey may have been used against civilians.

'The PKK, which seeks to establish an independent Kurdish state in south-eastern Turkey, accuses the Turkish government of waging war against its Kurdish population. Human rights groups have confirmed claims that the Turkish military has levelled hundreds of Kurdish villages and that in recent years hundreds of thousands of people have moved from the Kurdish East of the country into the major cities of Western Turkey. The European Parliament is sending a delegation to Ankara to investigate the accusations.

'The US coastguard boarded a …'.

Robert turned the radio off. There was nothing new under the sun. He only listened to the news because it was an old habit and because it lulled him to sleep. Years ago that was different. He would have become incensed at Turkey's high-handed violation of international law and disregard for human rights, and he would have identified strongly with the suffering of the people to whom he was called. Not any more. Politics now left him cold and he had hardened himself against the suffering of the poor wretches on the receiving end of Turkey's tender mercies. A man would go nuts if he tried to carry the burdens of the world. That was God's responsibility.

Once upon a time, years ago, he had aspired to be a famous Kurdologist. He did research, wrote articles for obscure magazines, taught seminars and showed slide presentations promoting the social and physical welfare of the Kurdish people. That was when he could still be moved by romantic notions about the liberation of the poor, the hungry, the oppressed. However, he'd lost those notions long ago, bitter experience having taught him that the Kurds were no better than their oppressors. Only their lack of resources kept them from behaving as cruelly to the Turks as the Turks treated them. The way the various Kurdish factions fought each other demonstrated they couldn't run a country if it were presented to them on a silver platter, as it was after the Gulf War. Let Turkey restore order so people can get on with their lives, he thought. Furthermore, shipping these people from their inaccessible mountain villages to the big cities was good for the advance of the gospel; now, instead of hiking for days up some mountain trail, he merely had to board a bus to arrive fresh as a daisy the next day.

He didn't aspire to become a famous Kurdologist anymore. He was content to be a modest missionary travelling throughout Kurdistan with the simple, profound message of justification by grace through faith in Christ's atoning death and resurrection. He had a vision of dozens of born-again groups of Kurds and Turks harmoniously worshipping God in Spirit and in truth. He could see these people in his mind's eye, their backs toward the world, their faces raised heavenward. Their inner peace and strength would be highlighted against the stark contrast of their society's evil ways and would be a testimony to God's redeeming power ... It was approaching 11.30 when Robert dozed off.

A distant rumble penetrated his sleep and woke him up. He peered at his watch and its luminous dial told him that it was just after 1am. The rumbling increased in volume until its vibrations rattled the window panes. He sat up, pulled back the sagging curtain, pressed his face against the glass and looked down the street. A convoy of huge flatbed trucks carrying German battle tanks on their way to Northern Iraq flashed in and out of the circle of light thrown by the street-lamp dangling from the wonky telephone pole.

The German minister of foreign affairs would lodge a formal complaint to his Turkish counterpart. Robert dropped the curtain, rolled back into bed and slept soundly.

Chapter 10

Masoud launched his long-planned business venture by trying to make a key-chain. First he bought a fancy, factory made one, unstitched it and traced its shape onto cardboard. Then he cut out the cardboard shape and used it as a template on one of his precious goat-skins. Holding his breath he cut it out. Then he soaked the piece of leather in water, folded it into the appropriate shape and let it dry.

The next day he mixed some binder and brown paint and brushed it evenly onto the shaped piece of leather. The paint took the rest of the morning to dry. That afternoon he brushed some leather varnish over the paint to make it waterproof and give it a nice shine. The varnish took the rest of the day to dry.

On the third day he assembled his hand press. Then he carefully punched two little holes into the leather and riveted the metal part with the dangling loops from which the keys would hang in its appropriate place. He punched a third hole in the centre of the outer flap and, using a pencil, made a mark through it into the bottom flap and made a fourth little hole. He unscrewed the bit from his press, screwed in a flat piece with a little bump in the middle and with a flourish fixed the snap-fastener in place. His first product was finished!

It looked and felt good. He turned it over and over in his hands and admired it. It didn't have the fancy stitching the factory-made original had, but then the factory ones sold for $4.50 while he would sell his for $2.50. He calculated that there was about 50 cents worth of material in his key-chains, so his profit would be two dollars a key-chain. He had to smile. Two dollars for three days work! However, tomorrow he would cut out and paint 20 key-chains, varnish them the next day and attach the metal parts on the third day. Profit would be $40 for three days work, and that was only the beginning! He would learn to make leather bags, belts and portable telephone cases. He would save up for a sewing machine and get Ayshe to help. Their future was sewed up in leather! He fondled his first key-chain lovingly, pulled a key from his pocket and slipped it onto one of the loops. Then he closed the flaps and tried to shut it. Oh dear prophet Mohammed, what now? He had attached the snap-fastener on up-side-down! He threw the key-chain onto the table and roared with laughter.

While his under-employed friends twiddled pens behind decaying government desks or gathered in the local tea-house to engage in futile denunciations of the latest government outrage, Masoud built up his little business. He learned to make leather bags by gluing the parts together, then marking off and punching a series of small holes through which he ran a hand-stitch. He made belts and got an order from a buggy driver for a new harness. Instead of using cardboard, he cut his templates from the flat sides of large, square, lard cans. He would spend a day or two cutting patterns, several days painting and varnishing and a day riveting the relevant metal parts into place. His work was displayed in several stores in downtown Hamadiye and he took his goods to Diyarbakir where vendors happily stocked it: his prices were competitive and his quality constantly improving.

He started putting money aside for a heavy-duty leather sewing machine. He also asked his parents to inquire about the availability of Ayshe.

One time, while on business in Diyarbakir, he noticed that the intense sunlight bleached the covers of books on display in bookstores, including the green and gold cardboard covers of the Qur'an. When he got home he made some leather Qur'an covers. On his next trip to the city he visited several book-stores with the faded Qur'ans in the window. The store-owners took the covers on assignment. They sold quickly and when he got back to Diyarbakir the following month he picked up orders for sixteen more covers. He made a whole stack of covers and peddled them at all the bookstores in Diyarbakir. That was how he became acquainted with 'The Professor's'.

Professor Baran was once a young, ambitious teacher of Sociology at the Tigris University of Diyarbakir. During the 1980 military coup, however, he lost his job and was put in jail, along with everyone else the military deemed left of centre. When he was finally released Professor Baran discovered that he was not welcome back at the University. Its staff and board of directors, if not its student body, had shifted decisively to the right in his absence. The professor considered his options, decided to borrow some money and bought an old, vaulted stone ruin near the university which, once upon a long time ago, had been an inn along the Silk Route. He bought, rather than rented, the place so the landlord couldn't be forced to throw him out. He had a mason repair the stone-work and a carpenter install bookshelves. He hauled in some couches and chairs, decorated the ancient place in a garish '60s-in-America style, and played music to match. One corner was rented to a former student, who invested in a large Samovar and served tea, coffee, beer and sandwiches.

'The Professor's' bookstore became the centre of gravity for the city's Bohemian subculture. Students, teachers, leftist journalists, impoverished writers, artists, musicians and those aspiring to be such congregated there to discuss the arts, to argue politics, and to talk about sex. It was, in fact, the only place in town where unmarried sexes met and mixed freely. This, of course, was enough of a reason for the city council's good Muslims to seek its closure. Professor Baran was, however, irrepressible. Each time the city council forced him to close his store he took the issue to court and each time he won, causing some to hint darkly about a leftist conspiracy in the judiciary. In time 'The Professor's' became, if not accepted, at least tolerated.

There wasn't much of a market for Qur'an covers at 'The Professor's', but going there became one of Masoud's little luxuries. The place was like a window into another world, a world distant from the loving but stifling traditions of Hamadiye. It reminded him of his lonely yet mind-expanding days in Istanbul and of glimpses he got of the West through imported TV shows.

Although Masoud didn't pretend to understand half the palaver spouted at 'The Professor's', didn't approve of the outrageous behaviour of some of the girls and knew he looked out of place twisting his prayer beads and wearing his baggy village trousers, he enjoyed sitting in a corner drinking a glass of tea, smoking a cigarette and eavesdropping on some discussion or other. He'd overhear the names of famous writers, philosophers, historians and theologians and he'd try to follow heated arguments about the applicability of their particular ideas to modern Turkish and Kurdish society. When his brain could take no more he'd squash his cigarette butt into the ashtray, get up and browse through the bookshelves until he found a volume with one of the names he'd overheard printed on the cover. In this way he built up his own eclectic little library. He wasted his money and mental energy on Hume and Hawkins, got bogged down in al Jaferi's commentary on the Qur'an, and tried to grasp Nietche, Hegel and Marx. He enjoyed Orhan Kemal, Orhan Pamuk and other Turkish novelists. He read translations of Naguib Mahfoud, Hanna Mina, Dostoyevski, Zola and Hemingway. Once he brought home all 22 volumes of an old, dog-eared encyclopaedia, built a shelf for it in his work place and, when he was tired of working, he'd pick a volume and read some article at random. Like much of 'The Professor's' clientele he gradually accumulated a confused collection of facts and fallacies. Unlike the others, however, he didn't assume anti-establishment attitudes. His little leather business was succeeding too well for him to be attracted to revolution and insurrection. Economic progress – even the mere hope thereof – is, after all, anarchy's greatest enemy.

Chapter 11

Robert woke up later than usual. It had been a late night and the elephantine curtains effectively shut out the daylight. He jumped out of bed, rummaged through his bag for soap and shampoo, grabbed the towel and headed down the corridor.

He was in a good mood; in spite of the soft mattress, his back felt fine. The shower stalls were dirty but the water, as promised, was hot. He kept the plastic hotel slippers on his feet while he enjoyed a good scrub. Then he dried himself and put his grubby travelling clothes back on. When he got back to his room he combed his hair and headed down the stairs to the lobby.

The man with the short, leftist beard was sitting at the check-in desk. He nodded politely as Robert walked by, lifted the phone and ordered breakfast from somewhere. Then he followed Robert into the lobby. It was empty. Robert went to one of the low couches beside the window and sat down.

Yesterday's newspaper was strewn on the table in front of him. He picked it up, shuffled the pages back into the right order and flipped through it slowly. The man with the beard sat down at his desk beside the opaque glass doors and picked his teeth with a toothpick. The muffled sound of traffic and the ululation from a distant radio heightened the brooding silence that filled the room. A police car, its blue lights flashing and its siren wailing, charged down the hill towards the intersection. A speaker crackled, the imam cleared his throat, then sang out the call to prayer, 'God is great. God is great. Come to prayer, come to prayer …' The tea-house door banged as the faithful shuffled off to pray.

A teenager carrying a breakfast tray pushed through the opaque doors. The man with the beard stood up, took the tray and with a curt nod dismissed the boy. Then he carried the tray to Robert, set it on the coffee table and sat down in front of him.

'Here's your breakfast, mister.'

'Thank you. Won't you have any?' Robert gestured toward the bread, olives and tea.

'No thanks, I've already eaten.'

Robert tore a piece off the bread, rubbed it in the butter and honey and started munching. The man with the beard watched him curiously, then cleared his throat.

'Do you know anybody here?' he asked.

'Not yet,' Robert said. He picked up an olive and popped it into his mouth. 'Great olives,' he added. There was an awkward silence, yet the man wouldn't be put off.

'Do you hope to get to know anybody here?' the man asked gingerly. Craning his neck exaggeratedly, Robert pretended to check that no one else was in the lobby. Then he leaned forward and whispered conspiratorially, 'How much does the secret police pay you?'

The man jerked straight in his chair. He was stung. 'I'm not police,' he said nervously.

'And I'm not interested in drugs,' Robert stated, looking the man in the eye. The man's face flushed. Then he stood up, turned on his heel and walked away. Robert watched him go. The man wouldn't cause any problems, but wouldn't help in an emergency either, he thought.

This little town was more difficult than he'd anticipated. If foreigners were automatically presumed to be drug dealers anybody he contacted here would immediately be in trouble. He sipped his tea thoughtfully, popped some more olives into his mouth, finished off the bread and stood up.

Back in his room he sat on the edge of his bed and fished his Bible from the satchel's side pocket. He tried to read, but couldn't concentrate on the words. His eyes glanced over the same passage again and again without grasping what it said. He closed the book and returned it to its side-pocket. It was always the same – after four weeks of trekking he was too burned out to concentrate on Bible study. Fortunately he was usually able to concentrate on his prayers by pacing up and down or by rocking his upper body and mumbling audibly. The room was too small for

pacing, so he moved to the edge of the bed and began
rocking forwards and backwards. He kept his eyes open and
stared at a spot of dirt on the floor. First he rocked until his
mind was clear. Then he mumbled his thanks to God that
his sins were forgiven, praised Him that he didn't have to
prove his spirituality by having to read his Bible when he
found it difficult to do so, told Him he needed wisdom and
strength for the day and reminded Him to take care of Inge
and the kids. After he finished his intercessions he continued rocking.

'If I have not love, I am a clanging cymbal.' Robert sat up
with a start. It was as if someone had addressed him from
within. It was some quote from the Bible.

'No love ... clanging cymbal.' I Corinthians 13. What did
that have to do with him? Surely nothing. He pushed the
disquieting verse aside and focused his thoughts instead on
mapping out the best way to approach his contact.

Chapter 12

During his second year in business Masoud bought the sewing machine. Since Alawite social structures are not as repressive as Shiite or Sunni streams of Islam, Ayshe was allowed to work the machine for him. She was a skilled seamstress and mastered the clumsy leather in short order. There was a steady demand for their sturdy bags, belts, Qur'an covers and key-chains.

By the middle of the third year he had paid off the sewing machine and by the end of that year had saved enough money to form the basis of an acceptable dowry. And Ayshe turned sixteen, the ideal age for marriage. His parents met again with his aunt and uncle, contributed to the dowry and settled the matter while his brothers and cousins helped build two adjoining cinderblock rooms to the rambling parental house. One room would become home for the new couple and the other room would house the sewing machine. It would become their new workplace.

The wedding took place in the spring. It was a memorable, fun-filled week of over-eating, music, dancing and story telling. The wedding night passed without incidence. Ayshe's mother received the bloodied bedsheet, proof of her daughter's virginity and guarantee of the family's honour, and waved it triumphantly before the boisterous crowd of well-wishers who had gathered outside the room while the wedding was being consummated.

Ayshe was a good choice for a wife. She was pleasantly plump and with an irrepressible fun streak. She had completed grade 4 at school, was a good cook, a superb seamstress and had a passion for cleaning. She fitted well into the family. Masoud's brothers and sisters treated her like an older sister and his parents like a daughter.

The business continued to grow and Masoud was able to employ his brothers. Young Bahadir helped in the workshop while Ayhan the playboy and Ahmed the religious one took their wares to Elazig, Mus, Bingol and Mardin. Ayhan and

Ahmed made a good marketing team: Ayhan concentrated on the secular and leftist clientele while Ahmed went to the religious ones. Masoud ordered raw leather in increasingly large quantities from Istanbul. He was saving for a second sewing machine and began dreaming of his own tannery. The flow of income and the employment were a source of hope to his previously discontented brothers. His position in the family was secure.

Now and again he and Ayshe permitted themselves a little luxury. They would take the early morning bus to Diyarbakir and, upon arrival, they would drink a glass of tea in the Eucalyptus garden next to the city walls. Then they would go their separate ways. Ayshe would head for the covered market and haggle over Iraqi tea or Syrian damask while he delivered some orders, collected some money or attended to bales of leather that had arrived from Istanbul and needed transporting to Hamadiye. He and Ayshe then met for lunch in one of the city's nice kebab restaurants. She would show him her purchases and he would tell her what he'd been up to. After lunch she would return to the covered market while he headed for 'The Professor's'. He would browse through the books, sit in a corner and glance at the piles of magazines and newspapers, or simply order a tea and enjoy the environment.

One day Professor Baran, who had noticed Masoud on previous occasions, introduced himself. Masoud's untainted, unaffected ways, his basic contentment with his lot in life, the sparkle of hope and success in his eyes, his appreciation for books, his desire to learn more and his initiative in establishing a leather business appealed to the jaded, worldly professor. He appreciated the distance Masoud had travelled single-handedly and, without saying as much, determined to help Masoud form a framework into which he could hang the disparate information he was garnering. The professor took time to discuss the things Masoud had been reading and tried to put them in perspective. Masoud's ignorance of Western history, however, was a large stumbling block.

One day the professor loaned him a copy of Fisher's History of Europe. It was a translation of the book's 1935 edition and its old Turkish was stilted compared with the English original, but Masoud couldn't know that. The book became the framework into which the fragmented bits of his previously garnered knowledge dropped into place. As he read and re-read the book he began to perceive something of the relationship between ancient Hellas, the Romans and the world of today. Philosophers and theologians he'd wasted his money on suddenly fitted into such related epochs as the Renaissance, the Reformation, Absolutism and Enlightenment.

Masoud grew to love history. Whenever he was in the big city he'd scour 'The Professor's' shelves, looking for history texts. The professor would loan him some books and Masoud would buy the ones he really liked. Thus Masoud's autodidactic education received a considerable boost.

Six months prior to the night Robert strode up the hill to the Aktamar Hotel, Masoud discovered a book in an obscure corner of 'The Professor's' with the intriguing title, The Balance of Truth. He picked it off the shelf, took it to a chair, sat down, ordered a tea and turned to the first page. The book was a translation of a work originally composed in Persian back in 1835 by a Westerner with the impossible name of Pfander. He looked at its chapter contents: The Testimony of the Qur'an to the Bible and its Trust-worthiness; The Attributes of God; The Fallen State of Man; The Way of Salvation through the Messiah; The Trinity; Does the Bible Contain Prophecies concerning Mohammed? Can the Qur'an be Deemed the Inspired Word of God? An Examination into the Life and Prophetic Office of Mohammed …

Masoud turned to the first chapter and started reading. The book, written in a lofty yet penetrating style, lucidly examined the commonly held suppositions which Muslims, including himself, held about Christianity. On the basis of the Holy Qur'an and easy-to-follow logic, the book not only answered each supposition, but also carefully crafted devastating attacks on the major tenets of Islam.

He suddenly put the book face down on the table and covered its title with his lower arm so that others couldn't see what he was reading. His mind was in turmoil.

Unlike most of 'The Professor's' other clientele, he did not espouse any counterculture notions. He was a faithful Alawite Muslim. He sincerely believed in God, in His prophet, and in the revelation of the Qur'an. He loved the caliph Ali, fasted, said his prayers regularly, loved his wife and children, did his work well, didn't cheat his customers and condemned violence and extremism. He enjoyed reading and learning – after all, the prophet himself had urged Muslims to 'seek knowledge, even if you have to travel to China to find it'. But this was different. This book, he realised, was dangerous. It attacked the fundamentals of all he held dear in a way the theoretical prattle around him never would. He felt like secreting the book back into the obscurity of its shelf in the far corner of the building. On the other hand, he knew intuitively that if he didn't explore the issues it raised he would wonder about them forever. He had come too far to remain happy in his ignorance. As he looked around at the few other customers lounging around him it dawned on him that if he dodged the real-life questions the book raised he'd become as empty as 'The Professor's' other clientele. The book would hound him if he replaced it. His eye fell on a label someone had pasted on the back cover. 'Those wanting to discuss the subjects covered in this book contact Robert Gauthier, P.O. Box 1289, Istanbul' it said.

Masoud waited until Professor Baran left the room, paid the somnolent student behind the cash register the price of the book, stuffed it inside his jacket and left.

Chapter 13

As much as his parents and Inge urged him to get a regular nine-to-five job at home, Robert knew he would never yield to that. After all, he had experienced The Call.

The Call to missions is an inexplicable mystery. It is impossible to explain its imperious nature to others. It is a mysterious, self-evident presentiment of truth in which the vanity and emptiness of normal domestic life overpowers a man.

The Call is like the turbulent force which drives the eel to repudiate its comfortable, tepid ditch to slither over ploughed fields, climb rocky barriers, and push through thorny hedgerows in search of the river which will take it to the open sea. Or it is like the magnetic compulsion which seizes geese at certain times of the year. Suddenly the petty concern for worms, grub and corn which once filled their little brains is displaced by visions of distant lands, expanses of salt water and turbulent winds. Just as the free and wild among them heed the mysterious call while their tame cousins, frustrated by fences and clipped wings, thrash futilely as they are gripped briefly by the knowledge of what life could be before sinking back into their apathetic, petty existence, so Robert had heeded The Call to fly wild and free, according to its dictates. He couldn't bear the thought of returning to the petty domestic concerns his family pressed upon him. The need for safety and security had crushed their ability to heed The Call. They were, he felt, even too dull to be tormented by the knowledge of what life might have been.

He, Robert Gauthier, wanted to live the life of the wild and the free, the life of one who has thrown off his shackles to follow The Call and live. He wanted to be counted among those who live because they deem their lives expendable, because they felt free to gamble with death. The sovereign truth of The Call, he felt, lifted a select few above petty realities to grasp the privilege of being used for eternal ends. The

Call breaks the bonds of perishable things for those who heed it for, like The Caller, they are prepared to live and to die for all men.

Chapter 14

Masoud was disappointed, irritable and restless. Although it was late and he was tired he couldn't sleep, and since his tossing and turning kept Ayshe awake he got out of bed and went to the living room. He turned on the TV and flicked through the channels for a while but other than senseless talk-shows there was nothing on. He picked up a book, but it was too deep for his tired mind.

The foreigner had broken his promise. All day today and all day yesterday and the day before he'd waited on tenterhooks for him, but he hadn't showed up. He should not have allowed his hopes to rise.

Masoud pulled the foreigner's letter from between two books in the bookcase and read it again.

Dear Mr Masoud Demirel,

Thank you for your kind letter. May the blessing of the God of all grace be upon you.

I was encouraged to read about your discovery of that disconcerting book, The Balance of Truth, and how it moved you to ask questions which few dare pose. Having the courage to question is a sign of spiritual vitality and mental vigour. It is the first step towards truth and, as Jesus Christ said, the truth will set you free – free from the bondage of sin, tradition and death. The unquestioning person remains a slave to his particular culture's traditions; that is why society resists the questioner – it doesn't want to release its slaves.

'Slaves of society' sounds like a harsh indictment, yet that is what we are. We are slaves of our controlling, dominating culture. Our families, mosques, teachers, friends and politicians turn against the lone, independent seeker who pursues his quest for liberating truth. They resist him because his questions condemn them. They resist him because his penetrating questions challenge the status quo's

offer of cheap security at the price of ignorance and falsehood.

The Balance of Truth has provoked you to ask questions. I want to warn you, however. Although there is a satisfactory answer to every honest question, those answers will stimulate you to ask yet more questions. In other words, you are embarking on a dangerous journey because truth does not reveal itself easily. This journey is not for the fainthearted, because they cannot withstand the animosity of family and friends which results when one breaks through the cocoon in which our community encases us.

Society made the Greek philosopher Socrates drink a chalice of hemlock because it couldn't stomach his questions, and it crucified Jesus Christ because it couldn't stomach his answers. Those who persevere, however, may be led step by agonising step to the source of eternal life, which is acceptance by a holy God.

The great Sufi poet and theologian Abd Allah Al-Ansari prayed,

'O God, seek me out of Thy Mercy that I may come to Thee and draw me on with Thy grace that I may turn to Thee.

'O God, I shall never lose all hope of Thee even though I disobey Thee, and my knowledge of Thy bounty has brought me to stand before Thee.

'O God, how shall I be disappointed seeing that Thou art my hope; or how shall I be despised seeing that in Thee is my trust?

'O Thou who art veiled in the shrouds of Thy Glory, so that no eye can perceive Thee! O Thou who shinest forth in the perfection of Thy splendour, so that the hearts of the mystics have realised Thy majesty! How shalt Thou be hidden, seeing that Thou art ever Manifest; or how shalt Thou be absent, seeing that Thou art ever present and watchest over us?'

God, the source of all life and truth, is the God of the free. He hides from those who are bound to sinful society and slowly, gradually, manifests Himself to those who throw off *the shackles which tie them to follow hard after what little light they have been given.*

Remember though that God is a jealous God. You cannot experiment with Him. If He chooses to reveal Himself to you He will never let you go again. He will hound you until you present yourself as a living sacrifice to Him. He will pursue you because his claim on you then will be stronger than society's claim on you now. Society's claim on you is that of a rightful slave-owner. God's claim will be that of Creator and Father. He will gradually re-mould you into His image and, step by step, give you real freedom, which is the power and will to do that which is right.

I will be travelling through your town toward the end of next month. If you are serious about seeking answers to your questions I shall gladly visit you before the end of the month. Simply mail me clear instructions on where I can find you. If you are not serious then you need not do anything. You will not hear from me again.

May the God of all truth scourge but receive you.
Robert Gauthier.

Masoud walked to the balcony, tore up the letter and, leaning heavily on the railing, let the bits of paper flutter away in the darkness.

Below him a military convoy carrying German battle tanks to Northern Iraq flashed through the circle of light in the town centre. He looked at his watch. It was just past 1am. The last day of the month had come and gone. He should not have allowed himself to believe that this foreign intellectual would stoop to visit him.

Maybe, he reflected, it was for the better that this man hadn't showed up. His letter inviting him had been a foolish impulse and he should be grateful nothing came of it. How could he have explained the arrival of this stranger to his family? He had been carried away by his modest success in business and assumed that his position in the family was secure enough to engage in foolish experiments.

Praise Allah that the man hadn't showed up. He would burn the book and stop visiting 'The Professor's'. God had kept him from foolishness.

Masoud turned around, headed back to his bed and stretched out on his back. His good intentions left him restless and uneasy. A phrase from the foreigner's letter kept flitting through his mind. 'We are slaves of our controlling, dominating culture,' the man had said. He is right, Masoud asserted. He stared for a long time into the enveloping darkness, then rolled onto his side and gazed at Ayshe's rhythmically breathing body. She was beautiful, he thought.

Chapter 15

After he'd finished his devotions Robert packed his satchel and returned to the lobby. He paid his bill, asked the man with the beard what time the evening bus to Diyarbakir passed through and headed down the staircase, through the door and out into the sunshine.

He looked up and down the street, then headed downhill toward the wonky street light. There was no point in trying to ascertain who was following him; they were much too good to be spotted. It wouldn't matter in any case. He made his way down to the intersection where he asked a traffic policeman for directions.

It was market day. Robert wove his way around stacks of fruits and vegetables, mounds of used and new clothing, endless rolls of textile and stacks of cheap plastic ware. Vendors shouted shrilly, old DeSoto trucks and Turkish-made Fiats jerked past. Old men bent double under grossly overweight loads plodded hither and thither, teenagers navigated heavily laden carts with reckless abandon through the crowd, old ladies with loads of firewood pressing them down waddled along like ducks on land, young men stood around aimlessly and followed Robert with suspicious eyes while countless kids in dull black school uniforms with dirty white collars deftly cut through the press, wielding their hard, plastic schoolbags as instruments designed for that purpose.

Robert threaded his way unhurriedly through the bustle until he reached a drab, grey, three-storey concrete building surrounded by rolls of barbed wire. In the space before the building's entrance a ragged hole appeared, as if by magic, in the constantly shifting human mass. No vendors' stands, no teenagers pushing carts, no trucks blocking traffic. Only blue-bereted soldiers carrying snubby submachine guns lounging against armoured cars or smoking cigarettes in one of several patrol cars parked with their doors open and their lights flashing. Robert headed for the gate. The person tailing him would have learned from the policeman that this was where he was headed.

Experience had taught him that it was better to deal with the military than the municipal police. Military personnel weren't local and were thus less likely to have personal axes to grind with the townspeople. Furthermore, their officers were much better educated and held more secular attitudes than the underpaid, undereducated local louts whose primary skills lay in handing out fines and racing around town in their patrol cars.

He told the guard that he wanted to see the officer on duty. The man, a muscular peasant with a face like a deflated soccer-ball, frisked him thoroughly, stared mutely at the foreign passport then looked up at him and grinned like an idiot. Although Robert addressed him in Turkish, the soldier insisted on communicating through gestures. Robert wondered for an instance whether the man was a deaf-mute, but then heard him shouting something to another soldier. Robert followed the grinning idiot into the drab, grey building. They walked down a hallway, up a staircase and down another hallway until they came to a yellowing, pock-marked door. The idiot knocked, then opened in response to a muted grunt.

A lieutenant wearing the red arm-band of the duty officer lay stretched back in an office chair, his feet on his desk. He was cleaning his fingernails with the tip of a bayonet. When he saw Robert he slid the bayonet in its scabbard, leisurely lifted his polished boots from between a pile of papers and some hard-covered notebooks arranged neatly on the desk, lowered them to the ground, straightened up in his chair and placed the bayonet where his feet had been.

The idiot saluted and responded to the lieutenant's raised eyebrow by explaining in a cultured Istanbul accent that the foreigner had arrived at the front gate, that he spoke fluent Turkish and had asked to see the duty officer. Robert looked at the man in astonishment. A slight nod from the lieutenant indicated that the soldier was dismissed. The man saluted smartly and backed out of the room, closing the door after him.

Robert stood at ease before the steel desk. For an instant he and the lieutenant looked into each other's eyes. The man was about his own age, Robert thought. He looked fit and alert. His uniform was immaculate, the blue beret folded neatly in his shoulder lapel.

'Parlez vous Francais?' The officer spoke slowly, deliberately, accurately. His voice was a pleasant tenor.

'Oui, un peus. Je suis Canadien,' Robert smiled disarmingly. 'However, I speak better Turkish than French.'

'Please sit down. You can practice your Turkish all day long, while there is no one here to speak French with. We'll use French.' The officer smiled.

Robert pulled up the straight-backed steel chair and sat down.

'I've lived here for 11 years and this is the first time somebody addresses me in French. People usually try German or English,' he said. 'Where did you learn French?'

The lieutenant smiled again. 'My parents were guest workers in Belgium. I was born in Liege. However, they returned to Turkey when I was twelve.'

'You have wise parents.'

An eyebrow lifted and the slight questioning shake of the head told Robert to explain himself.

'You might have become another second-generation immigrant with an identity crisis.' Robert smiled disarmingly.

'C'est possible.' It was difficult to tell whether the lieutenant was piqued or amused. 'What can I do for you?'

'I came to visit an acquaintance. Since we're in the special security zone I thought it might be best to report to you before getting myself into trouble.'

'What kind of trouble do you expect?'

'I'm not expecting any, just avoiding it. I can appreciate that this is an unusual destination for a tourist. Also, I haven't the faintest idea where this man I'd like to visit lives, and hoped you might be able to help.'

'The traffic police would have obliged.'

'C'est possible.' Robert raised his eyebrows slightly, shrugged his shoulders and made a disarming gesture. The lieutenant was sharp, suspicious, ambitious, potentially dangerous, potentially useful. Robert enjoyed fencing with him.

'Who is this friend of yours?'

'I have never actually met him. I'm a free-lance writer and this man, a certain Masoud Demirel, responded to something I'd written. His letter intrigued me. He appears to be something of a home-grown intellectual – his questions, at least, were reasonably intelligent. Anyway, I promised him that the next time I travelled through I'd pop in to see him.'

The lieutenant listened with his elbows leaning on the desk, his hands pressed together and his chin resting on his finger tips.

'What kind of things do you write about?'

'I try to make the world of Islam intelligible to Westerners and the Christian world to Muslims. I cover such subjects as language, culture, long range developments, religious sects and beliefs.'

'Can I see something you've written?'

'Sure, but I don't carry my portfolio around with me,' Robert grinned. 'Here's my card. If you're ever in Istanbul …'

Robert pulled his wallet out of his pocket and extracted a business card. He then pulled a mechanical pencil from his breast pocket and scribbled an address on the back. The writing was barely legible on the high-gloss paper. It smudged easily and would soon be altogether illegible. He handed it to the lieutenant, who examined the professionally designed and printed card carefully. Robert Gauthier, free-lance writer and translator, it said. There was also a Post Box in Istanbul and an E-mail number. The Post Box belonged to a friend. The lieutenant placed the card on his desk. He appeared satisfied.

'Care for a glass of tea?' he asked.

'Don't trouble yourself.'

'You're not in a hurry are you?'

'Not really. If possible I'd like to visit this Masoud before getting on the evening bus to Diyarbakir.'

'It is still early. A tea, and then one of my men will take you to your friend.'

'That's very kind.' Robert's vague reply could have applied to either the tea or the offer of being escorted to Mr Masoud. The lieutenant reached for an invisible button and pressed it. A soldier entered promptly and saluted.

'Mohammed, two teas.'

'Yes, sir.'

As they sat sipping the hot, sweet liquid, Robert had to suppress his delight. Without knowing it the system had lost another little battle.

'Is your friend expecting you?'

'I wrote that I expected to travel through Hamadiye towards the end of the month. I don't suppose he's expecting me anymore.'

The lieutenant pressed the button again. Mohammed reappeared and stood smartly at attention while the lieutenant explained what he wanted. The soldier saluted and left. After a few minutes he re-appeared and stood at attention behind Robert. The lieutenant rose from his chair and extended his hand.

'Enjoy your visit, Monsieur Robert. If I can be of further service, you know where to find me.'

'Merci beaucoup pour tout, et au revoir,' Robert said as they shook hands.

Mohammed escorted Robert to the front gate where a jeep stood waiting for him. The idiot grinned and beckoned him from behind the steering wheel.

Chapter 16

The workshop buzzed with activity. Masoud was cutting patterns for leather bags using tin templates, Ayshe was teaching one of Masoud's sisters how to sew the pieces together, and Ahmed sat behind a little metal desk composing a list of which stores in which cities had ordered which items. Ayhan, squatting on a low stool strategically located in the doorway, was looking and winking at passing girls.

'Masoud, look at this list.' Ahmed held up the paper.

'Can't read it from here, what does it say?'

'The orders from Siirt, Diyarbakir and Mardin. You know, it is getting really difficult to haul all this stuff around by bus.'

Masoud had to smile. His brothers had broached the subject of purchasing a vehicle before.

Ahmed put the paper back onto the desk. 'With a vehicle we'd be able to expand to Elazig, Tatvan, Bitlis, Van, even as far as Erzurum.'

Masoud didn't reply, concentrating instead on the bag he was cutting.

'You know Masoud, Ahmed is right.' Ayhan leaned forward on his little stool and tried to look serious. 'We really should get a vehicle soon. We could ship a lot more stuff. It would soon pay for itself. What do you think?'

Masoud had, in fact, given the subject lots of thought and had made up his mind. He knew the state of their finances, how much money's worth of leather goods they produced and when they would be able to buy the second sewing machine which would justify the loan for the van he had in mind. However, he couldn't merely state his intentions and get on with it; that would appear dictatorial and would drive his family against him. He had to lead his brothers, each of whom had different ideas about how their profits should be spent, to a consensus, and that consensus had to be what he had in mind from the start. It was a wearisome process.

'When we were in Diyarbakir I saw this nice little Mazda for sale,' Ayhan continued hopefully. He had visions of himself impressing the girls of Hamadiye with a slick sports-car.

'What good is a little Mazda?' snorted Ahmed. 'A good, used bus is what we need.' He dreamt of organising trips to Mecca for the annual Hajj and to Konya for the December Mevlana festivities and to Urfa, the city of the prophets, and to other religious sites around the country.

'It has a strong engine. It could easily pull a trailer. You could use it for both work and pleasure,' Ayhan insisted.

'I've been thinking about a vehicle myself,' Masoud inter-rupted. The other two looked at him with renewed interest. This was the first time Masoud had let himself be drawn into a discussion about a vehicle.

Masoud looked at Ayhan and scratched his eyebrow. 'It's true that we would be able to distribute much farther afield. The problem is that we can hardly keep up with the orders we're getting. Before getting a vehicle we've got to get another sewing machine. When both Ayshe and Hatije are sewing we could probably justify a vehicle.'

Just then a military police jeep came careering around the corner at the bottom of the street, changed gear, and stormed up the hill.

'Military police coming,' Ayhan said. 'I wonder who they are looking for.' The others fell into an uncomfortable silence as they waited for the jeep to pass their quarter.

'It's slowing down,' Ayhan reported. 'He's looking for someone around here.' The others responded with uncharac-teristic silence. Masoud and Ahmed headed for the door. The sewing machine ground to a halt and Ayshe and Hatije waited nervously.

The jeep slowly approached the workshop, then stopped. A large soldier with a punched in face leaned out the vehicle's half-sized door.

'I'm looking for someone named Masoud Demirel,' he shouted. He spoke with an Istanbul accent.

Ayshe put her hand to her mouth to stifle a cry. Ahmed and Ayhan looked at Masoud in fear. Masoud felt his knees going weak.

'I'm Masoud Demirel', he said. His voice was wavering.

'Good. I've brought you a guest.' The soldier turned to someone hidden in the shade on the passenger's side of the vehicle, said something and shook that person's hand. That individual opened the jeep's door, stepped out and looked over the top of the vehicle. He was tall and lean and had a longish face. Nonchalantly he threw a foreign looking satchel over his shoulder, looked up and down the street as if trying to get orientated, then nodded at the three men standing at the workshop door.

'Hello. My name is Robert Gauthier. Sorry I'm late.' He spoke with a trace of an accent. His voice had a warm, pleasant tone to it.

The soldier with the punched in face revved the jeep's engine, did a U-turn and waved goodbye. They watched him go. Then Masoud let out a long, slow breath, stepped forward and held out his hand.

Chapter 17

The soldier had driven Robert back into town, up the hill, past the hotel he'd stayed at and into a warren of dirt alleys and ramshackle buildings. They had to stop twice to ask for directions. Countless eyes followed the jeep's progress from shadow-filled doorways. Even if he himself felt vaguely uneasy, however, the soldier beside him seemed to be perfectly at ease.

They eventually found the right street and drove up the hill until they came to the workshop. The sign over the door said, 'Demirel Leather Works'.

He got out of the jeep, thanked the driver and told him he'd make his own way to the bus station that evening. A young man who claimed to be Masoud Demirel came out of the shadows when the jeep disappeared and held out his hand.

'Welcome,' the man said. His voice quaked a bit. Robert could see that he was unnerved. He probably thought the military police was going to haul him off to jail, Robert thought, smiling to himself.

He took the man's outstretched hand and shook it. 'Thank you very much. I'm sorry I'm a bit late,' he said. He looked carefully at his host. The man had the typical long, lean Kurdish features. He wore a clean dress-shirt and the baggy shalwar trousers favoured by villagers. He sported a black moustache and, in spite of his receding hairline, looked like he was only in his mid-twenties. Robert thought he could see the dull fear lingering in his eyes.

'No problem. I'm honoured with your visit. Please, come in.' The man looked flustered for a moment, then pointed at the other two men in the shop and said in a distracted way, 'These are my brothers Ayhan and Ahmed.'

Robert shook hands with the two younger men. One had the greased-back, slightly out of style look of the country dude; the other had all the accoutrements of the Islamic fundamentalist: sunken cheeks, black, piercing eyes, mousy beard, skullcap, drab, oversize clothes. The Dude hailed him heartily, kissing him on both cheeks as though they were long lost friends, while the fundamentalist extended him a cold, lifeless hand accompanied by a long, suspicious look.

'I'm pleased to meet you both. My name is Robert.'

The Dude ushered him into the workshop and with a gesture and a gentle shove lowered him onto a low stool.

'How are you, Mr Robert? Where do you come from?' he asked. The guy smelled of cheap cologne.

Robert didn't answer him right away. He had to get a feel of the place first. He lowered his satchel onto the floor, leaned his forearms on his upper legs and looked around him. The shop, permeated with the typical stuffy, pungent smell associated with leather, was about twenty square metres in floor area. In one corner stood an old-fashioned, heavy-duty Singer sewing machine. Two young women were hunched behind it. He noticed that one of the women got up in response to a rapid series of signs from Masoud and left the room by a back door. She lowered her head and looked at the floor as she passed the men. That must be Masoud's wife, Robert thought, and she was just told to prepare a meal. The other, younger, girl followed her out.

Several bundles of leather were stacked around the place. Judging by their size some of the skins must have come from sheep or goats while the thicker, larger pieces must be cow-hides. Some of it was painted, some of it was cut into various shapes, some of it sewn together into various half-finished articles. In one corner stood a table with open pots of black and brown paint. Beside it was a second table with a pile of finished products on it. Robert stood up and walked over to it. He looked at the key-chains, leather bags and book-covers which were drying on it. The products had a rough-and-ready, sturdy look about them. It was the type of stuff the urban environmentalist, the support-native-craftsmen crowd at home would like, he thought.

'Nice, good quality stuff you make.' He looked at Masoud, hoping to shake the Dude from him.

'Thank you.' Masoud's voice still sounded weak. The poor devil still hasn't recovered from the shock, Robert thought.

'Please, sit down. Would you like something to drink?' The man was rediscovering his voice.

'Don't trouble yourself. I can't stay long.'

'A Coke? A glass of tea?'

'A glass of tea would be nice. Thank you.'

'Ayhan, get tea, will you?' The Dude slipped out the front door, leaving Robert with Masoud and Ahmed. Masoud was gradually re-gaining his composure. His breathing returned to normal and the tense lines in his face relaxed.

Ahmed sat down behind the little steel desk and gazed disapprovingly at him, something which didn't bother Robert. He was used to the hostile stares and heated, politicised arguments of fundamentalists. They didn't annoy him anymore. No matter what he did or said they would not see him as an individual human being. He was a Westerner, even if from a harmless country, so he represented the 'evil, imperialistic West, the Great Satan'. And, by virtue of the Bible he read, he was doubly dangerous. He was deluded and a potential deluder of the pure but naive children of Islam.

When he turned away from the table with the finished products on it to go back to his stool Robert noticed a shelf with books behind the steel desk. He sauntered casually around the desk toward the bookshelf, putting his hand on Ahmed's shoulder as he eased his way around the back of his chair. He felt the man stiffen. Robert smiled inwardly. There is nothing like physical contact to reduce the level of hostility. Physical contact and a joke. His sense for humour had eased him out of many a tight spot before.

He looked at the books on the shelf. They were a dog-eared mixture of Western classics and modern Turkish novels as well as some history and sociology and a faded encyclopedia set.

Bingo, he thought. I've found him again; the local, homegrown intellectual. The questioning man, the man who has become frustrated with the strictures of his family and society, the man for whom there is a faint hope for eternal life.

He returned to his stool. Masoud sat down beside him. Robert looked him in the face and smiled.

'Well, its good to meet up with you. Are you the owner of this workshop?'

'Yes I am. Thank you very much for coming. I didn't think you would come.' Masoud began to unwind.

'I got held up in Elazig. I'm glad to meet you. I won't be able to stay long, but I was determined to give you this present.' Robert reached into his bag, pulled out a New Testament wrapped in brown paper and handed it to Masoud. Masoud accepted it gingerly and put it aside. He suspected he knew what it was and didn't want to open it in Ahmed's presence. He would deal with the consequences of receiving this visitor and his gift later.

The Dude returned with the tea. Two other young men trailed after him into the shop; a bunch of kids started to collect around the doorway. Ayhan placed the tray with the tea glasses on the desk.

'Sugar?'

'Two please.' The Dude handed him two lumps of rock sugar. Robert dropped his two in the glass, Masoud and Ahmed stuck theirs between their teeth and lower lip. They sipped quietly for a while.

'Mr Robert, we are honoured with your visit,' the Dude said. 'But what brings you all the way here?' Even the Dude was suspicious.

Robert was used to suspicion. People here had every right to be suspicious. They were caught in the vice of harsh military law on the one hand and brutal insurrectionists on the other hand. These people had learned long ago not to trust anyone outside their family.

'I am a writer and researcher,' Robert replied loud enough for anyone to hear. 'Mr Masoud and I have been corresponding and I promised to visit him the next time I travelled through.'

There was a stir among the young men as they digested this information. They threw suspicious glances at both him and Masoud. Ahmed looked stoneyfaced.

'What kind of things do you write about?' The Dude had appointed himself as spokesman. Masoud became tongue-tied again; this time he was afraid to incriminate himself against his family.

Robert realised that Masoud had not told anyone about the possibility of his coming. That was normal. People either didn't really believe that he would come, and didn't want to make fools of themselves by claiming something as preposterous as a visit by a foreigner, or they didn't know how to tell their families that they'd been communicating with a stranger. In either case people simply tended to hope for the best when he did show up.

'I try to make the world of Islam intelligible to Westerners and the Christian world to Muslims. I cover such subjects as language, culture, long-range developments, religious sects and beliefs.' Robert repeated his standard answer.

'Are you a Muslim?' It was the first time Ahmed opened his mouth.

'No. I am a Christian.'

This caused another stir among the listeners. He was the first Christian they had ever met in person.

Masoud straightened up in his chair. He was moved to defend himself.

'I found Mr Robert's address in a book. I wanted to find out what Westerners thought about the prophet Mohammed, God bless Him, and the Holy Qur'an. The prophet said, "Seek knowledge, even if you have to travel to China to find it", so I wrote a letter to Mr Robert.' He had found his tongue all of a sudden.

'Mr Robert then wrote me back saying he was passing through Hamadiye and would be prepared to stop by for a visit.' Masoud turned to Robert. 'Welcome to Hamadiye, Mr Robert.'

Robert grinned while Masoud shook his hand a second time. The formalities, always tense, were over. The tension and suspicion were still there but, against all the odds, the Kurds' irrepressible sense of hospitality won out once again.

Chapter 18

The foreigner had dark brown, wavy hair which fell forward, framing friendly yet piercing brown eyes. His face was longish and the rest of his body was tall and slim. He wore jeans, a khaki shirt and good quality walking shoes. Masoud suspected that the man was in his mid-thirties. He spoke flawless Turkish but with a slight, lilting accent. He was too lean to pass as a Turk, Masoud thought, but he could be mistaken for a Circassian, or even a wealthy Kurd. There was an air of freedom, of not being beholden to anyone, about him. He looked like he would be at ease anywhere and in any company, Masoud thought with a sudden flash of envy. He, on the other hand, had to consider his family's wishes with respect to everything, even though it was he who had built up the leather business! Surely it was up to him to decide who he corresponded with and invited over for a chat!

They were sipping tea in the shop. The fear had dissipated somewhat and the atmosphere was more relaxed. Even Ahmed seemed to let his curiosity get the better of his suspicion.

Word about the foreigner whom the military had personally delivered to Masoud spread rapidly through the quarter and the workshop filled with curious men. The foreigner sat comfortably on his stool in the middle of the crowd and answered their questions.

'I learned Turkish at the University of Istanbul, where I studied Middle Eastern languages and Islamics.'

'No, I am not a Muslim. I am a Christian.' This again caused a ripple to run through the crowd. He was the first infidel any of them had ever spoken to. The man seemed quite comfortable with his infidel status, however, and answered their questions in his own imperturbable way.

'Why am I not a Muslim? As I mentioned, I studied both Islam and Christianity in depth. Don't get me wrong: there is much about Islam I admire. However, with respect to some things it teaches the exact opposite of what the Bible teaches.'

Masoud saw Ahmed lean forward. 'That's because the Bible has been changed,' Ahmed said.

'Has it really?' Although the foreigner smiled at Ahmed, there was a cool, confident, challenging look in his eyes. Masoud sensed his brother's hackles rising.

'Yes. Priests have removed every reference to Mohammed, God bless him and grant him salvation.' Ahmed was fingering his prayer beads furiously.

'Let's cover one topic at a time,' the foreigner said. 'Firstly, in what way does the Bible differ from the Qur'an and secondly, are those differences the result of priests changing the Bible or not?' The crowd nodded, curious as to how the infidel would answer these imponderables. They were safe because their man Ahmed had studied these things and would argue on their behalf against this man's heresies.

'Without doubt the greatest difference between the Qur'an and the Bible is their incompatible description of the person and work of Jesus Christ, peace be upon him. According to the Qur'an, he was one of the greatest prophets, right?' The men, taking their cue from Ahmed, nodded.

'According to the Qur'an Jesus Christ, peace be upon him, was born of a virgin, taught the word of God, and was taken up into heaven, right?' Again everybody nodded.

'However, according to the Qur'an he didn't die, did he?' the foreigner asked.

'Do you believe that Jesus Christ, peace be upon him, was the son of God?' Ahmed burst out.

'We'll get to that in a minute. Did Jesus Christ die on the cross or not?' The foreigner looked at Ahmed with those cool, piercing eyes of his.

'And because of their saying: We killed the Messiah Jesus, son of Mary, Allah's messengers – They did not kill or crucify him, but it appeared so to them; and look! – those who disagree concerning it are in doubt about it; they have no knowledge of it except pursuit of a conjecture; they did not kill him for certain; but Allah took him up to Himself. Allah was ever mighty, wise,' Ahmed replied intensely, quoting Sura 4:157-158 from memory.

'Well done,' replied the foreigner. 'So the Qur'an clearly denies Jesus Christ's crucifixion. Now tell me, who would the jury in a court of law believe: the eyewitnesses to an event or someone who came along more than six-hundred years later and told some story which was the exact opposite of what the eyewitnesses claimed had happened?' The men, even Ahmed, remained silent. They weren't sure what this was leading up to.

'Obviously, any court of law would rule that the testimony of eyewitnesses carries more weight than that of someone who showed up six-hundred or more years later in a totally different place with a totally different story,' the foreigner continued, looking around the sea of faces which had gathered around him.

'The Bible is the testimony of eyewitnesses – lots of them – to the person, work, death and resurrection of Christ. Here let me read you a few verses.' The foreigner reached into his satchel and fumbled around until he found a little cardboard box. Inside the box was a little book with the words, 'New Testament' printed in embossed gold on the cover.

'That book has been changed,' Ahmed said contemptuously before the foreigner could find the passage he was looking for. 'It's testimony isn't valid.'

The foreigner put the book back into its little box and carefully placed the box on the table. Then he slowly, deliberately turned those brown, piercing eyes toward Ahmed.

'Tell me, when was this book changed? Before or after the time of Mohammed?' The foreigner pointed toward the little cardboard box with the forbidden book in it. His voice suddenly had a penetrating ring to it. The man's refusal to say 'God bless him and grant him salvation' after saying Mohammed's name had a jarring effect.

Ahmed was about to say something when he checked himself. It suddenly dawned on him that the question was loaded with ramifications, though he couldn't quite identify them. Silence lay for a long, heavy, uncomfortable instance in the air. With no reply forthcoming the foreigner continued speaking.

'If you believe that the Bible was changed before Mohammed's time you violate the teachings of the Qur'an. It clearly teaches in such passages as Sura Il-Kahf verse 26 that God's word cannot change. In fact, the Qur'an goes much further! Passages such as Sura Al-i Imran verses 3 and 4, state that the Bible is light and guidance and that the Qur'an came to verify it! In Sura En'am verses 91 and 92 it not only states that the Bible is light and guidance, it repeats the fact that the Qur'an came to verify the Bible. Sura el Maide, verses 46 to 48 state once again that the Bible is light and guidance and that it is unchanged.' The foreigner ticked the Quranic verses off his fingers and spoke rapidly.

'The Qur'an verifies the trustworthiness of the Bible and goes on to proclaim judgment on those who judge it.' Then his piercing eyes once again zeroed in on Ahmed.

'Be very careful in your judgment of the Bible, God's eternal word,' he said with a grave, almost ominous, finality.

Chapter 19

Robert was thoroughly enjoying the challenge of religious debate. The arguments these people put forward were nothing but variations of the hackneyed themes they had been taught in primary school: priests had changed the Bible, excising any reference to Mohammed in the process. Christians hold to the abhorrent, blasphemous notion that God Almighty once had intercourse with a woman and thus produced a son. They also believe in an absurd, incomprehensible doctrine called the Trinity and insisted that God let one of his prophets, Jesus, die the accursed death of crucifixion at the hands of the Jews. The more erudite might suggest that St. Paul was the villain who re-interpreted – and corrupted – original Christianity. Robert had long ago worked out and memorised answers to most of the common issues. The challenge lay in devastating the opposition's arguments without damaging his sense of honour, so that he would have a chance to give a coherent gospel presentation in the end.

He loved the primitive dynamic of arguing with Muslims on their own harsh turf. He hadn't noticed any mosques when he and the Idiot had driven through the quarter, which led him to believe that these people might be Alawites. This Ahmed was evidently not merely the most religious of the lot, but was apparently also the self-appointed defender of Islamic orthodoxy. If they were Alawites this Ahmed's heavy-handed approach to religion probably wasn't shared by most of these guys. On the other hand, they were probably more xenophobic than the normal Sunni Turks or Kurds. He would have to discredit this Ahmed without being excessively aggressive. Fortunately, the man set himself up as an obvious target. Once he'd neutralised him he would be able to get on with the job of presenting the gospel of the forgiveness of sin and of eternal life through faith in Jesus Christ. Communicating that simple message was

what it was all about. It was the driving force behind The
Call.

Robert lifted his sombre gaze from Ahmed and looked
around the circle of men.

'Do not judge the Bible,' he repeated. 'In doing so you
call God a liar.'

'Then the Bible was changed after Mohammed's time,'
Ahmed blurted out defensively.

'By the time of Mohammed there were countless copies
of the Scriptures – even today there are thousands of Bible
manuscripts scattered in museums all over the world which
pre-date Mohammed and the Qur'an. Muslims can go and
look at these manuscripts in the museums of Rome, St
Petersburg, Paris or London if they so please. There they will
also find ancient translations of the Bible in Latin, Greek,
Coptic, Gothic, Syriac, Ethiopian, Armenian and Georgian
which go right back to the second century. If, as you claim,
someone or some group tried to forge the Bible sometime
after the 7th century, they would have had to find and
change every single copy of the Bible. If a single copy in any
of these languages escaped falsification, their efforts would
have been in vain.' Robert spoke rapidly, clearly. He knew
that his audience was only barely able to follow his reason-
ing, but that didn't matter. The only thing that mattered was
convincing these people of the trustworthiness of the Bible
and demonstrating the weak position of their Muslim apol-
ogist.

'Even if someone managed to accomplish this massive
fraud, it would have been exposed by the recent discovery of
very ancient manuscripts which had been considered lost
long before Mohammed's time,' he continued. These could
not possibly have been corrupted after his appearance. They
are no different from this copy of the Bible here on the table
in front of you.' Robert pointed once again to his New
Testament.

'The word of God stands for ever. A Muslim who truly
believes in the Qur'an will not be misled by the prejudices
of his ignorant society but will obey the Qur'an's teachings

and take the Bible as his light and allow himself to be guided by its teachings. To do this it is necessary to study it prayerfully, praying in all sincerity that God Most Merciful will grant him wisdom to understand its teachings and give him strength to walk according to its precepts.' Robert's voice dropped off. He knew he was starting to walk on thin ice. He had to devastate without being antagonistic. Nor could he push abstract, Western logic any further with this audience or he would lose them. He could see them starting to fidget and murmur among themselves and his real target, Masoud, wore a pained expression on his face.

Robert turned once again toward Ahmed and let a warm smile break across his face.

'Ahmed,' he said, 'I didn't notice any mosques on my way here. Are you Alawites?'

Ahmed winced. The others nodded.

'Tell me about your beliefs.'

Chapter 20

The eclectic Alawite religion goes back far in time. Although it draws its name from Ali, the son-in-law of Mohammed, the founder of Islam, Alawite religious customs exclude many of the practices of orthodox Islam. They are, in fact considered a non-Islamic cult by orthodox Sunni Muslims.

Alawites practice their religion in secret, although their villages are easily identifiable because of the absence of mosques. Their rites involve progressive initiations through which the novice ascends by degrees into the inner knowledge of the sect. As he progresses, he is gradually accepted into the community's ruling oligarchy.

No one knows how many Alawites there are since they pretend to adhere to the dominant religion of the area in which they live in order to escape persecution. Some say that up to twenty-five percent of the population of Turkey and six percent of the population of Syria is Alawite. Most of the Alawites in Turkey are either descendants of the Southern Arabian tribe of Nusayr, which emigrated to the region of ancient Antioch, or are Kurds who live in the mountainous region between Elazig and Bitlis. Mountainous regions have always been breeding grounds for religious heterodoxy.

Although Alawite beliefs and practices vary somewhat from group to group, their teachings include vestiges of the astral religion of Babylon, including the belief that the Milky Way is made up of the deified souls of true believers. They hold to Gnostic and dualistic notions passed on to them by the Ismailis and practice certain typically Christian rites, such as a form of baptism and the celebration of Christmas, which they gleaned from the Armenians. Some Alawites believe in re-incarnation. They also practice the Persian religious feast of Newroz.

They hold that God is the supreme being, and that emanations of God are always present in the world. In the past such emanations included prophets, mystics and men with miraculous powers such as Noah, Moses, Mohammed, Ali, the Twelve Imams and the Muslim saint Khizir who gained immortality by drinking the water of life. Jesus Christ is also regarded as a prophet. Some even hold that he was, in some sense, divine.

In short, this beleaguered religious/ethnic group, which shuns legalism and holds that what a person is in his heart is much more important than outward religious practices, has absorbed elements from all the religions which have passed through their remote mountains since Hellenistic times. Of all Muslim people groups they are considered the most responsive to the Gospel, although their tight, hierarchical, clan-based social structures form a tremendous barrier to expressions of individualism which a personal faith in Jesus Christ demands.

Some of Islam's greatest Sufis, men such as Haji Bektash Veli and the mendicant poet Yunus Emre, who was consumed by the love of God, were Alawites.

Chapter 21

Masoud slipped out of the workshop and trotted across the courtyard of the family home to make certain everything was under control. It was.

Ayshe had killed, gutted and plucked several chickens and they were floating in seething pots of boiling water. She was stirring rice, nuts, currants and various spices into a bowl of butter and broth when Masoud entered the room, while one of his sisters was folding scallions and dill into a pan with chicken livers. Another sister had spread a table-cloth on the floor and was arranging cushions around it. Although everything appeared in order, Masoud worried the ladies by poking in their pans, fluffing up already fluffed cushions, chasing a stray child from the living room and straightening a picture on the wall. Ayshe eventually shooed him out of the house. She told him to come back with his guests in an hour.

Masoud hurried back to the shop. The crowd had grown even larger. Those nearest the foreigner were squatting or sitting down and those behind them were leaning forward so that they could see and hear the man even better. Masoud noticed that his father was standing quietly near the door, peering through the crowd. He made his way over to him.

'Who is this man?' his father asked.

'A foreigner I've corresponded with. He is a writer. I saw his name in a book I was reading.'

'And he came all the way here just because you wrote him a letter? What does he want?' His father sounded suspicious.

'I'm not sure what he wants. He offered to stop by on his way to Diyarbakir. I didn't really expect him to do so, but here he is!'

'What kind of things does he write about?'

'He tries to make Islam understandable to Westerners and Christianity to Muslims.'

Father and son stood together and looked at the foreigner for a while. The man was responding to some query about the Trinity.

'Of course the teaching of the Trinity is impossible to understand. That's the beauty of it. You Muslims have your God all figured out: He is one and these are his ninety-nine characteristics. We Christians cannot reduce our God to understanding. That is why He is worthy of our worship. If we were able to understand the essence of our God, as you claim you do of your God, He would, in my opinion, not be worthy of my worship anymore. God would have shrunk to my puny ability to understand Him. A God who is that small is not worthy of my worship.

'God is a Triune God,' the man continued in his solemn, lilting voice. 'Three in one, one and three, one God in three persons. He is God the Father, the creator of all things, God the Word made flesh in Jesus Christ, and God the Holy Spirit who is at work exposing sin, revealing the way of salvation, and drawing you toward Him. Don't try to understand. Simply fall down and worship. ...'

The foreigner's clear, slightly accented voice rang through the shop as he said the last sentence. The men stirred uncomfortably, then began murmuring once again among themselves. Masoud's father looked distressed.

'This foreigner is a troublemaker,' he murmured. 'He is...' he searched for the right word.

'He is ...' suddenly it dawned on the wise old man. 'The man is a missionary!' he spat out with disgust.

The lights suddenly went on in Masoud's mind. Of course! That was it! The man was a missionary! Once in a while there were programmes on television about men like this, Western agents who sought to influence public opinion in Islamic countries so that its people would become more pro-western.

'Dad,' he whispered. 'I've got to invite him to stay for dinner. Please come,' he pleaded.

'I'll have nothing to do with that man. He is trouble.' His gentle father turned on his heel and walked out of the shop.

Masoud watched him go with a sinking heart. Why had he invited this missionary? Who had he thought himself to be to invite this stranger over to spout his dangerous poison without consulting the family? The thought that he had unwittingly invited a missionary into his home almost made him sick. However, there was no turning back now. Praise Allah, the man had indicated that he wanted to catch the evening bus to Diyarbakir. This nightmare would end soon, though not soon enough.

Chapter 22

'Let me tell you a story that will explain the point about the importance of the Bible,' Robert was saying. 'Once upon a time there was a rich man who lived in a house which had four beautifully furnished rooms. One evening, as he was reclining in the first room, a thief climbed through a window right beside where he was lying down. When the thief saw the rich man he nearly turned and ran away. He noticed, however, that the rich man didn't react to his intrusion. In fact, there seemed to be a dullness about him. The thief thought that maybe the man was retarded. So, resisting the urge to run, he proceeded to fill his bag with valuables, all the while keeping a careful eye on the motionless rich man. When the thief had filled his bag he climbed back out the window and disappeared.

'The following evening the thief returned, breaking into the second room. Again he ran into the rich man, and again the rich man just gazed passively as the thief proceeded to strip this even more beautiful room of its valuables. Again, when he had filled his bag with valuables, he left. On the third evening the same thing happened in the third, most beautiful room of all.

'When the thief entered the fourth room on the fourth night, however, he was surprised to see the rich man sitting in an empty room among a few worthless rags. This time the thief scampered boldly around the room to see if there might be any treasures hidden somewhere, but he couldn't find anything. Out of frustration he kicked the bundle of dirty rags the rich man was sitting on. Who can describe the thief's astonishment when the rich man reacted furiously to his touching those rags! The man pounced on him and threatened to kill him if he ever touched his precious rags again! The thief ran for his life, utterly bewildered.'

'What is he trying to say?' Robert overheard someone asking.

'I think he just said that the Qur'an is a worthless old rag,' someone replied.

There was an uneasy stirring in the room. Robert smiled. They'd gotten the point.

'Don't you see,' he said, seeking to drive the point home. 'That rich man is no different from your God. He didn't mind when people ruined the Tevrat, the book of Moses, nor when they ruined the Zebur, the book of David, nor when they ruined the most beautiful book of all, the Injil, the book about Jesus. But when someone touches that fourth book, the Qur'an, the book of Mohammed, he becomes furious. What kind of God is that?'

Masoud pushed his way through the crowd. Robert saw him coming and thought he looked strained. Had he pushed his luck too far, he thought briefly. That parable of the rich man was a powerful one …

'Mr Robert, won't you come for dinner?' Before Robert could make the requisite excuses Masoud had grabbed him by his elbow and had pulled him off his stool. The crowd opened silently before them as they headed for the back door, the Dude and Ahmed following after them. The rest of the crowd filtered out onto the street muttering among themselves. Whatever happens next, Robert thought, this has been a good visit. I've communicated truth to these people. Let them discuss what they've learned and draw their conclusions as a community. If I could communicate the gospel message as well, this visit would be complete.

The brown package Robert had handed to Masoud earlier lay forgotten on the table.

Masoud led Robert through the leather-shop's back door and into the courtyard of the family's dwelling. They crossed it and walked over to his and Ayshe's room. He didn't dare entertain his awkward guest in the larger family room after his father had voiced his disapproval.

Masoud was nauseous with anxiety. On the one hand he wished he'd never invited this man to come; his main concern now was to discharge his duties as host as best as he could and then get rid of him as soon as possible. The entire town from the Military Police on down to the street urchins knew he was in contact with a foreign missionary, a foreign spy. First of all he had to get him away from the crowd and into his own house. There he would feed him and then he would accompany him to the bus stop and see him off. There would, undoubtedly, be rumblings in the family for a while, but that would subside in time. He would never make contact with this man, or anyone like him, again. It was too dangerous. He simply couldn't afford to lose all he had built up so carefully.

On the other hand, he was angry with his father and brothers. Even if the man was a missionary, he hadn't done anything wrong. He had asked for permission to come and what he said made sense. The authorities obviously didn't think he was a threat or they wouldn't have delivered him to the door! The man was surely right when he wrote about the tyranny of one's family, Masoud thought. His father and brothers were behaving shamefully. He wished he were able to talk to the man in private.

When they came to the room they took off their shoes and he ushered the foreigner to the place of honour, in the centre of the mattress, the place farthest from the door and surrounded by cushions.

The foreigner, Ayhan, Ahmed and Masoud squatted cross-legged around a plastic table cloth spread out on the floor. Ayshe placed several dishes filled with pistachio nuts, almonds, salted pumpkin and watermelon seeds and several small bowls of rock sugar on the plastic sheet, then carried in the typical two-part Turkish tea-pot. Masoud first poured a bit of the strong brew into the glasses from the top pot, then thinned it to the required strength with hot water from the lower pot, and passed them around, beginning with Robert. Masoud and his brothers sipped their tea through the rock sugar between their teeth while the foreigner dropped his cube into the tea glass and was left searching for a teaspoon. Masoud made a nervous gesture and Ayshe came scurrying with the desired item.

The conversation lagged into an uncomfortable silence. Masoud kept a close eye on the tea-glasses, refilling them when they were close to empty.

Eventually Masoud collected the glasses and handed them to Ayshe. She soon reappeared lugging a round tray piled high with rice, pine-nuts, aubergine, and spiced chicken. Then she brought in a pile of plates which Masoud filled to overflowing and handed to his guests.

The men lifted their spoons and turned towards their plates. A joyless silence hung in the air. There was no giggling pile-up of small, shaven heads and laughing, naughty brown eyes in the doorway and there was no titter emanating from the women in the kitchen. Only the quiet crunching sound of mastication disturbed the ominous silence.

As they ate Masoud became increasingly irritated with his family. These people, he thought, just took, took, took. They took the work he gave them, took the money he gave them, tried to take decisions about the future of his business from him, and now took away the joy of entertaining a foreign guest.

Suddenly there was a stir in the hallway and Ayshe appeared in the doorway gesturing nervously. Masoud jumped up and headed for the doorway, to reappear a moment later ushering in Uncle Mehmet's massive bulk. Both his brothers and the foreigner shuffled to their feet while Uncle Mehmet nodded and smiled. His brothers moved toward the man to kiss his hands, but he told everyone to sit down and carry on. The men were careful to sit slightly down from where they had been sitting, so there would be room on the cushion in the place of honour. However, after shaking hands with Uncle Mehmet, the foreigner promptly sat right back down in the seat of honour. Masoud had a moment of panic but, wheezing and puffing all the while, Uncle Mehmet lowered his massive bulk at the foreigner's right side. Ayshe appeared with another plate which Masoud filled to overflowing.

Robert sensed that the huge man beside him was important in this community. He briefly thought of offering him the seat of honour, but decided against it. He sensed a groundswell of hostility to his message. The fact that – besides this obese, wheezing hulk beside him – only Masoud's younger brothers joined in the meal spoke volumes. They were here merely to keep an eye on him and on their older brother. Where was the rest of the family? Where were the older men? And who was this fatso? Somehow he didn't think he was Masoud's father. They wouldn't have tried to kiss his hand if he had been.

In any case, he felt that he couldn't afford to lose the high ground. By retaining his seat of honour he sought to communicate that he was not to be messed with, that he was important in his own right, that he had connections in high places. Whoever this huge man was, he was no more than a local dignitary.

'Do you speak Turkish, son?'

Robert looked up at the man's use of the word 'son'. The huge man had grabbed a chicken leg and was peering over it. He too was jockeying for position, Robert thought. If he replied 'Yes sir', he would have established the fact that the man was more important, so he instead he said, 'Yes I do, Mr – what was your name?'

'Mehmet,' the man replied amicably

'I studied Turkish in Istanbul, Mr Mehmet.'

'What brings you to Hamadiye, son.'

Robert wished the man would stop calling him son.

'I came to visit our host, Mr Masoud.'

'And how did you get to know Mr Masoud?'

'He wrote to me and I offered to visit him when passing through town.'

'What did Mr Masoud write to you about?'

Robert felt like telling this fat slob that that was none of his business. He noticed that Masoud was looking very miserable. This fatso could find out from Masoud himself what he wanted him to know, he thought. Robert turned and looked the man in the eye. The little pupils peering from the creased folds, somehow reminded him of shivering little oysters wallowing in their slime.

'Mr Mehmet, if you want the details of Masoud's personal correspondence, ask him,' Robert said with an aggrieved air. 'Why don't you tell me a bit about yourself,' he continued. 'Are you Masoud's father?'

'No, I'm his uncle. ... You are a missionary, aren't you?' A dangerous mist clouded over the oyster-eyes.

Robert didn't bat an eye. Instead he put his spoon down and gazed with mild disgust at his interrogator.

'No, Mr Mehmet,' he said, 'I am not a missionary.' Robert had said this simple statement often enough and in suffi-ciently different contexts that he could say it with just the right amount of conviction.

Denying he was a missionary used to make him feel guilty. It used to make him feel like he had just told a lie, but that was not the case any more. The word meant one thing to his supporters and his home church, and a totally differ-ent thing to the average Muslim. To folks at home the word referred to someone going overseas to spread the message of the gospel; to the Muslim the word missionary was synony-mous with Western spy. To them missionaries were foreign agents who sought to turn people against the established order. They turned son against father, daughter against mother, husband against wife. They weaned people away from the moral standards of Islam and introduced Western ways and Western morality. The word had two different meanings, and he, Robert Gauthier, was not what they asso-ciated with the word missionary.

'I'm not a missionary,' he repeated, 'but praise God, I am Christian, a follower of Jesus Christ. Religion is a subject of eternal importance and as such demands our earnest atten-tion.'

An uneasy quietness settled over the meal. Masoud attended to his painfully few guests. He bravely doled out generous quantities of food until his few guests moved their plates from in front of themselves, covered it with their hands and said a closing blessing.

When everyone had had enough they all sat back, rubbed their distended stomachs, belched, grunted and murmuring blessings on the family. Ayshe reappeared, collected the tray and hauled it off to the kitchen so she could eat the left-overs later.

This Masoud fellow will never invite me back, Robert thought. Whatever I can communicate I've got to do now. 'Lord,' he prayed, 'give me a chance to share the gospel message. I don't want these people's blood on my hands. Allow me to leave in peace.'

Ayshe lugged in trays of peaches, plums, pomegranates and grapes. Masoud handed small plates and knives all around.

'Let me tell you a story which sums up the essence of what we Christians believe.' Robert decided to take the initiative. The men looked sullenly in his direction.

'Once upon a time there were two brothers, the older God-fearing and the younger a rebel,' Robert pressed on. 'One day the younger brother lost his temper, and in his anger killed someone. After that he ran home, stripped off his bloodstained clothes, and put on his older brother's clean shirt and trousers and hid somewhere. 'When the older brother came home and saw the gory clothes lying on the floor he realised what had happened. He quickly jumped into those bloodstained clothes just as the police arrived. Then he, the older, innocent brother was arrested, tried, found guilty and hanged.

'Afterwards the younger brother became terribly convicted about the wrong he had done. Not only was he a murderer, his crime had led to the hanging of his saintly brother! Full of remorse he went to the judge and confessed all. The judge gazed at him, then told him it was against the law to punish the same crime twice. Since his brother had paid the required penalty he, the guilty one, was free.

'The younger brother couldn't believe his ears. His brother's innocent blood had bought him his freedom! Thereafter he determined to pattern his life after the self-sacrificing love of his brother, and dedicated the remainder of his days to reaching out to his former cronies.'

Robert stopped briefly to let the impact of the story sink in. Then he continued. 'Do you understand?' he asked, looking around the little group. I am the younger brother and Jesus the older brother. Instead of accusing us, Jesus offers us his robe of righteousness. He put on my blood-stained clothes and was hanged in my place. Since my sins have been punished God, the judge, sets me free. That is the message of the Injil, the book of Jesus.'

Robert noticed the look in Ahmed's eyes. They were filled with hate. ...

Chapter 23

Masoud pecked at his meal in silent self-reproach. He should never have invited this foreigner to visit him. Success in business and his more secure standing in the family had caused him to become too proud, too sure of himself. He should have known better than to take individual initiative. What had the foreigner written in his letter? We are slaves to our family. He was right! We are slaves. This was his guest, yet he had not been able to speak a sentence with him in private. He longed to see this foreigner go, yet he also longed to spend a few minutes in private with him. But even if he could get a few minutes alone with him, what would he say? They couldn't continue communicating after this. Corresponding was out of the question … or was it? Maybe if the letters were not sent to the house. But where to then? There wasn't a soul in Hamadiye whom he could trust to pass on the man's letters unopened. Who could he trust? A safe address. A place his family knew nothing about.

Masoud racked his brain. Then it dawned on him: 'The Professor's'! If the foreigner sent his letters to 'The Professor's', Professor Baran would certainly hold them for him until he came to Diyarbakir to pick them up. That was it! But how could he communicate this to the foreigner. Was it even worth it? The man was right. He was a slave to his family and his family was selfish and ignorant and he was left with unanswered questions. If he didn't seize this chance, then he would never forgive himself. This foreigner, whoever and whatever he might be, cared enough to visit him. You couldn't help but admire him. He cared! How was he to know his family wouldn't accept him? But the man did know – he had said as much in his letter.

A note. If I could slip the man a note with 'The Professor's' address on it, Masoud thought. It would be dangerous …

In the course of the meal Masoud became obsessed with the idea of writing a note. He also became increasingly worried again. He could tell that Ahmed was livid and might do something that would get them all into trouble with the authorities who had, after all, delivered the man to their door. He couldn't leave until the conversation had moved to something lighter, until the atmosphere was less oppressive. 'Dear Allah,' he prayed, 'let me slip out of the room long enough to write this man a note.'

'You know, I've always wanted to emigrate,' Ayhan said suddenly. 'How does one obtain a visa for your country?'

'I wouldn't know,' the foreigner replied amicably. 'I have a Canadian passport, so I don't need a visa.'

'I've heard that if someone sponsors you they will give you a visa,' Ayhan persisted.

'That may be true for some countries. I haven't the faintest idea what the visa prerequisites are for my country.'

'I've heard that if a Muslim becomes a Christian you people give them money and help them go to the West,' Ayhan continued.

'True religion is a personal relationship with God,' the foreigner replied. 'You don't need to go to the West to have a relationship with God.'

'Are there Muslims who become Christians?'

'Yes, a growing number.'

'Is it true that if a Muslim becomes a Christian you help him emigrate to the West?'

'No, that is not true.'

'Then why would a Muslim want to become a Christian?'

'In order to obtain eternal life,' the foreigner said with finality.

There was another strained silence. Then Ayhan said, 'Which country do you like better, your own or Turkey?'

The foreigner smiled. 'There is much about Middle Eastern culture in general and Turkish culture in particular which I appreciate. However, I think everyone loves his own motherland in a special way, don't you?' There were involuntary nods of agreement.

At that moment Masoud could have kissed his little brother on both cheeks for changing the subject of conversation. The heavy atmosphere lifted somewhat. This was his chance. He shuffled to his feet and was just heading for the door when Ahmed popped a question which made his heart skip a beat.

'Do you support the Kurdish war of liberation?' Masoud turned to see how the foreigner would handle this one.

'The Kurdish war of liberation is a Kurdish affair. The subject doesn't interest me and I have nothing to offer those who pursue it. My concerns are eternal.'

Masoud saw Uncle Mehmet purse his lips at this response and at the same time saw the foreigner look questioningly at him as he made for the door. He smiled and nodded back and saw the foreigner smile back as though he understood that he was about to do something important. Then he slipped out the door and was away.

He jogged across the courtyard toward the workshop, pushed the door open and looked around. There was no one there. He sat down behind the desk and reached into a drawer for a pen and paper; then eyes fell on the forgotten package the foreigner had given him. He ripped the brown paper off it. It was, as he had suspected, a book. The New Testament it said in gold letters on the front cover. His heartbeat increased as he held the much maligned book in his hands. He slipped it behind a row of books in his bookcase.

Then he quickly grabbed the pen, ripped a page out of a notebook and wrote:

> *Dear Sir,*
> *Thank you for coming to visit us. I would have liked to spend some time speaking with you in private, but that is not possible. I do have a number of questions and will write you. However, please do not write back to me at this address. Please note the address of 'The Professor's' bookstore in Diyarbakir and send any future correspondence there. I will ask them to hold letters addressed to me. Thank you for your visit.*
> *Sincerely,*
> *Masoud Demirel.*

Masoud folded the piece of paper, shoved it into his breast pocket and headed back to the meal. He hoped that the others merely thought that he had gone to the toilet.

Chapter 24

Robert was ready to go. He felt that there was nothing more for him to do here. He was disappointed that he had been unable to speak to Masoud but, on the other hand, he had communicated as much truth as these people could cope with. He had discharged his obligations; the next step was the responsibility of the Holy Spirit.

He felt heavy hearted, but then he always did after he had shared his heart with people who responded by raising their hackles or by asking the inevitable stupid questions about which country was better, his own or Turkey, or by inquiring how one could obtain a visa for the West.

The Turks' complex psychology seemed to have blinded them to the inconsistency of their two most common questions. They craved the constant re-affirmation that their country was the best, yet no one was more eager to leave it. They suffered from a strange mixture of inferiority and superiority complexes over Westerners.

He glanced at his watch. It was approaching five o'clock. The bus would pull into town after dark, at around seven o'clock. Two hours to go. They were finishing up the fruit now. After that tea would be served once again and then he would be able to make his escape. He would have to communicate his intentions as soon as Masoud returned from wherever he had gone – probably to the bathroom, though that would be unusual. People here would sooner burst their bladders than dishonour their guests by leaving them unattended during meal time. Had Masoud really gone to the toilet? He had smiled that enigmatic smile before slipping out of the room. What was the man up to?

Just then the door opened. Masoud re-entered and resumed his seat beside him. He was followed by the young woman who collected the dishes with the fruit skins and peelings on them. This was the moment. Robert looked at his watch.

'The bus to Diyarbakir leaves in about an hour, doesn't it?' he asked. If they confirmed that, then it was clear that they wanted to get rid of him as soon as possible.

'Yes, but you must spend the night with us,' Masoud replied. Etiquette demanded that he make the offer, just as it demanded that Robert refuse it.

'Thank you for your kind offer but I must get home,' he said. 'My wife and children are waiting for me,' he added.

He regretted saying that as soon as it had slipped out of his mouth. No self-respecting Turk would appear to let his schedule be dictated by his wife and children. He sensed a ripple of mirth flow through the huge hulk beside him, and saw the disdain in the Dude's and the Fundamentalists' faces. Somehow or other, however, he didn't think that Masoud shared their disdain.

'As you like,' he heard Masoud say gently. 'But you are welcome to stay as long as you want.' Although the offer was repeated, the lack of insistence and the insipid way in which it was communicated indicated clearly that he was not really welcome.

'Let's drink a glass of tea and then I will accompany you to the bus station,' Masoud continued.

That was a good one, Robert thought. This Masoud knew as well as he did that the bus didn't leave until seven, yet he offered to accompany him right away to the bus station. Normally he would have expected to stay until just prior to the bus' departure. How many times, in similar circumstances, had he wondered whether or not they would make it in time? This Masoud was up to something, Robert thought.

The young woman who had collected the plates returned with a tray of tea glasses and the double pot of tea. Once again an uncomfortable silence settled over the room. Everyone was engrossed in his private thoughts as they sipped their tea.

The man with the mousy beard, the Muslim fundamentalist finished his glass of tea, stood up and with a curt nod toward Masoud left the room. Robert noticed that the Dude was looking at him from the corner of his eyes while still sipping his tea. It looked as though he was still trying to figure out how he could get to the West.

Robert slowly finished his tea and placed the glass on its side on the little saucer. Masoud did the same. Suddenly it dawned on him what Masoud was after. He wanted to escort him to the bus station in the hope of getting away from his family! He looked at Masoud and with a little jerk of his head communicated that they go. It would be rude, it would be abrupt, but it was the only way. In any case, the Fundamentalist's sudden departure would make his leaving look less abrupt. The others would be sure to stay for second and third cups of tea, while Masoud might reasonably be expected to escort his guest. Masoud responded with a wan smile and nodded his head slightly.

Robert jumped up in response. 'Thank you for your hospitality,' he said to everyone. 'You have been very kind …'

'It's still early,' Ayhan said. 'Have another glass of tea.'

'No thank you. I must get going. To get to the bus station I simply keep walking downhill until I get to the main street, turn right and head for the intersection, where I turn left, right?'

'I'll walk you over there,' Masoud said almost too eagerly.

'Don't trouble yourself,' Robert said. His heart leapt with joy. 'I can find my own way easy enough.' It was going to work!

'No, I'll walk you over,' Masoud replied evenly.

Robert walked around the room and shook hands with those that were left. He left the fat slob till last. The little oyster eyes followed them suspiciously and Robert was glad to get into the courtyard. Masoud came after him carrying his satchel, and led him through a steel door to the street outside. Once outside Robert let out a long, relieved sigh. He heard Masoud do the same thing. They looked at each other, then burst into nervous laughter.

Chapter 25

They walked in silence until they reached the end of the street. When they turned the corner Masoud took hold of Robert's elbow in an almost involuntary demonstration of intimacy.

'Do you know 'The Professor's' bookstore in Diyarbakir?' he asked. 'It's where I found the book with your address in it.'

'I know the place. I slipped several copies of that book onto the bookshelf, praying that God would lead people in whom His Spirit was working to them.'

They walked quietly for a moment, then Masoud said, 'I must have bought the last copy. ... It is a troubling book.'

'I hope the book and my visit haven't caused trouble for you.'

'My family doesn't know about the book.' They walked quietly for a few minutes. 'It is a dangerous book and caused me to ask many fearful questions,' Masoud continued. 'I am afraid of my questions and, worse, don't know where to go for answers.'

Robert didn't reply immediately. His heart was heavy, as it always was when he had led his contact to the crossroads. If he could just walk out of Masoud's life now the damage his visit had caused would be temporary. Masoud would be able to pick up his life and would soon be re-accepted as a member in good standing within his community and extended family. He would expand his little business and employ some other family members. He would have children with that sweet little wife of his who had served them so diligently. He would live as happily as could be expected. ... But only if he, Robert Gauthier, simply walked out of his life forever, right now.

But he knew that he would not walk out of Masoud's life, just as he hadn't walked out of a dozen of other men's lives whose existence was now, humanly speaking, ruined. Almost a dozen men in almost a dozen years who had followed his advice, who had kept on asking questions, who had placed their marriages, their jobs, even their lives on the line in order to learn and live by the truth of the gospel. The price of eternal life is high, he mused. God always chooses the hard way, the way of the cross.

His mind flitted to a harrowing scene he had read recently in a book by the Japanese novelist Shusako Endo, where a Portuguese missionary was forced to watch as Samurai warriors tortured and killed Japanese Christians. The Samurai swore they would keep on killing Christians until the missionary renounced his faith. He, who was prepared to lay down his life for others, was forced instead to watch others lay down their lives for him. That too, was part of The Call, Robert mused.

'Masoud,' Robert said, 'If you want answers to your questions I will happily correspond with you. In fact, we run a correspondence course that deals with the questions you are asking. If you want answers to your questions I will see to it you get that course. But I warn you once again: those who ask questions free their minds from the shackles placed on them by their society. By attempting to break out of those shackles you are running a great risk,' he stated sombrely. 'But the reward for those who persevere is eternal life,' he added.

'You must not come here again.' Masoud reached into his shirt pocket and pulled out the slip of paper with 'The Professor's' address on it.

'Here is 'The Professor's' address. Please send that course there. Don't send anything here.' Masoud hesitated briefly, then added, 'You must not visit me here again.'

'Don't worry, I only visit people upon invitation,' Robert replied. 'I will happily meet up with you anywhere else. Maybe we can meet sometime at 'The Professor's' and talk at leisure.'

'You would come all the way from Istanbul to meet with me at 'The Professor's'?'

'Yes.'

'Why?'

'Because of what is at stake: freedom from sin, the strength to do what is right, eternal life …'

They continued to walk silently down the hill until they turned the corner at the wonky telephone pole. As they did so Robert looked back and saw Ahmed following them.

'Don't look behind you, but one of your brothers is following us,' he said.

'Which one?'

'The one with the beard. Just walk with me to the station, say farewell, turn around and go home. Don't wait until the bus comes.'

'That would be dishonourable to you.'

'Don't worry about me.'

They walked silently to the dusty, dun coloured parking lot of the South-East Bus Company and Robert bought a ticket to Diyarbakir. They shook hands.

'Thank you for coming,' Masoud said.

'Thank you for inviting me. Your brother is watching us from the other side of the street. Just walk over to him and return home with him. You will hear from me via 'The Professor's'.' Robert looked into Masoud's eyes and saw that they were filled with a mixture of fear and determination. It was the look typical of a Muslim whom the Spirit had chosen for eternal life, he thought.

He watched Masoud leave the little office and cross the road. He saw the startled expression on the Fundamentalist's face when he realised he had been caught spying on his older brother. He saw Masoud put his arm around him and walk back into town with him. Neither of them looked back at him.

Robert looked at his watch. It was six o'clock and the light was fading. He sat down on a bench in the unlit cinder-block and corrugated iron waiting room, put his elbows on his knees, rested his head in his hands, closed his eyes and gently rocked back and forwards. He rocked until his mind was clear, then he mumbled a prayer of intercession on behalf of Masoud. He went on to pray for himself. Inge was waiting. He couldn't postpone returning home any longer. He would need strength and grace. What had he told Masoud? That the gospel offered freedom from sin, the strength to do what was right and eternal life.

'If I have not love, I am a clanging cymbal.' Again that insistent inner voice addressed him and the words reverberated through his head. 'No love ... clanging cymbal ... clanging cymbal ... you're a clanging cymbal, a resounding gong.'

The words piqued him. No one ran greater risks for the sake of the gospel and no one communicated it as eloquently as he did. He tried to suppress the voice but the words came back and had a sharper edge. 'Do you love Inge ...? ... clanging cymbal, a resounding gong ...' The words pierced his defenses and bore into his being. They probed and searched until they located a remote and calloused place buried deep within his psyche. He was impotent while the words discharged their full, convicting power: 'You don't love Inge as you ought to ... you're a clanging cymbal, a resounding gong ... you're a proud and arrogant man ...'

He buried his face in his hands and tears welled up in his eyes. 'I know,' he whispered. 'Oh God, be merciful to me. Grant me the love I lack.' As he mouthed the words cathartic spasms convulsed his shoulders and the wetness flowing freely down his cheeks began its cleansing task.

By the time the bus finally descended the ravine into town it was dark.